A
Harlequin
Romance

WELCOME

TO THE WONDERFUL WORLD

of Harlequin Romances!

Interesting, informative and entertaining,
each Harlequin Romance portrays an appealing
love story. Harlequin Romances take you
to faraway places — places with real people
facing real love situations — and
you become part of their story.

As publishers of Harlequin Romances, we're extremely
proud of our books (we've been publishing
them since 1954). We're proud also that Harlequin
Romances are North America's most-read
paperback romances.

Eight new titles are released every month and are
sold at nearly all book-selling stores across
Canada and the United States.

A free catalogue listing all available Harlequin Romances
can be yours by writing to the

HARLEQUIN READER SERVICE,
M.P.O. Box 707, Niagara Falls, N.Y. 14302.
Canadian address: Stratford, Ontario, Canada.

or use order coupon at back of book.

We sincerely hope you enjoy reading
this Harlequin Romance.

Yours truly,

THE PUBLISHERS
Harlequin Romances

A SCENT OF LEMONS

by

JILL CHRISTIAN

HARLEQUIN BOOKS   TORONTO
WINNIPEG

Original hard cover edition published in 1972
by Mills & Boon Limited, 17-19 Foley Street,
London W1A 1DR, England

© Jill Christian 1972

Harlequin edition published January, 1973

SBN 373-01651-4

Printed in Canada

1651

CHAPTER ONE

RORY McDERMOT, having nothing to hurry for, stood on the small quay watching the high-prowed caique unload. He had shared the three-hour voyage from Kyrenia in Cyprus with an oddly assorted cargo which included two flop-eared goats and a bright scarlet bicycle, and felt some interest in identifying the consignees. His human fellow-passengers had been met noisily and affectionately by friends and families, and had repaired with them to the wooden chairs under the vine-shaded verandah of the *taverna* on the quayside.

Later, Rory promised himself, he too would retire to the shade of the *taverna* and trickle a measure of fiery ouzo down his throat. But there was no hurry. The Mediterranean sun was warm on his back, not yet too hot.

The island smelled sweet. The water was turquoise clear and he could see small fish darting in the shadow of the gaily painted caique. The paint was sun-bleached into soft hues, though the staring open eye on either side of the prow had been renewed lately.

He let his glance travel slowly along the quayside houses, and beyond to the rest of the village which straggled a short way up the hillside and ended in olive groves. All the houses were white, with red pantiled roofs and outside stairs. There was a shop, with neither window nor door; just a three-sided room where the proprietor sat on a wooden chair in the midst of his wares.

A small excitement twisted in his breast. This might be the place he was looking for. If that Greek waiter

5

was right, and the house by the monastery could be bought, this might be his home for the foreseeable future. He drew in a deep breath, relishing the herby scent, the sharp lemon blossom in it, and woodsmoke. A man might live on the island well enough, and have no need of what they called civilisation which had grown so uncivil of late; and if he behaved himself and walked doucely, in time he might come to be accepted by the inhabitants.

He was not unaware of eyes watching him. Of course they watched a stranger. In his boyhood in Connemara, the arrival of a stranger had meant two days' excitement and chatter. Slowly, he lowered his backpack to the warm white stones, and turned a little to let them see him, as was friendly. Later, they would want to know his name and business, and maybe they'd ask or maybe not; but he knew what was due to a village and would let them know, obliquely or direct as they preferred it.

Out of the corner of his eye he saw two girls. One dark and plump, a typical Mediterranean young woman you could see anywhere from Crete to Anatolia. Dark, plump, inviting; a quick-ripening beauty already with a hint of the fatness to come. The other?

He held his breath and turned carefully, to see her better without seeming to stare. Where on earth did *she* come from? She was a beauty—slim, fair, delicate-boned, holding herself proudly and aloof. A goddess, risen like Aphrodite from the foam of the sea? Yet she wore the usual drab black garment of no particular style, which he'd seen on women of all ages and sizes lately. In it, she looked as graceful, as elegant, as a young queen. Her hair shone pale gold and her skin was like pearl. B'golly, he thought with a sudden grin at the fancy, I'll be writing poetry before I'm much

6

older. And it wasn't for women I came to this place, or any place. Anyway, she's a child, no more.

Suddenly there was a good-natured cheer, which brought his attention back to the caique. A big square-built man held a red bicycle high above his head, and a small fair boy danced on the quay with excitement.

'Hi, Georgi! Here it comes! Watch out, I'll throw it.'

The boy squealed, 'No, don't. Don't throw it! It'll get broken.'

The men laughed. The fair girl appeared by his side as if by magic, and her voice rang out. 'He's teasing you, Georgi! Wait now, I'll help you.'

The island patois was Greek basically, but with a twist of its own which made it hard to follow. So far, he had only understood the boy and the girl clearly, but coming across, the boatman had understood his own careful, bookish Greek sufficiently. He would manage, and he had a quick ear and tongue for picking up words.

It was Georgi's birthday. The girl's name was Evie, and she was his sister. The pair of them were not out of the island basket, that was plain to see. Yet not strangers or visitors. They were accepted by everyone.

A touch on his arm took his attention from the brother and sister. It was the dark girl, who introduced herself as Sofia. 'You're welcome to the island, sir. Is there anything you want to see particularly? That's the monastery, up there through the pepper trees. You can go up by the river if you like. Or there's the church. Maybe you'd like to take a photograph, or drink some coffee?'

He experienced a sudden sense of delight, a feeling of homecoming. A conviction that he had not met the Greek waiter by chance, and that the house would be for sale, as the Greek had hinted. His dream would come true here. It had started already.

'Coffee,' he told the girl. 'My name is Rory. I come from Ireland.'

She frowned, not quite understanding his painstaking Greek. 'Today? Is that in Cyprus?'

'No, no. I was born in Ireland. Today from Cyprus. Last week from Athens. The week before, from—'

The dark head nodded firmly. Now she understood. 'You are a tourist,' Sofia told him. He bent his head, not daring to contradict. Some day he might know the words to explain to her that a tourist had some place to go home to; that he had none.

Instead he told her he was hungry. The golden girl had disappeared, with the boy and the shining bicycle, and he was sorry for it. He wanted to look at her again, having a feeling that a man might look at that lovely withdrawn face a long time, and not tire of looking. But she had gone and it was a long time since breakfast, and the sea always made him hungry; even the gentle summer tideless Mediterranean, so far and so different from the cold sea which crashed for ever below the black cliffs of Moher on the far west coast of Ireland.

Sofia took his hand and led him to the *taverna* as if he had been a blind man, though it wasn't twenty paces from where they'd been standing. She shouted in a shrill fast dialect into the back of the inn, and a man's voice answered. And presently the man himself came out of the shadows through a shabby flowered cotton curtain carrying two plates; one laden with bread and green olives; the other with dates and goat cheese. Not what Rory would have chosen if asked, but he accepted the assortment with a murmured thank-you. He had learned to enjoy fish and chips in England and hamburgers and corn on the cob in the States. He

8

stood no nonsense from his taste buds. They took what he gave them, and had to be thankful.

Evie and Georgi Marsden were obliged to push the bicycle when they came to the end of the village road and started to climb up to their home. There was no proper road up to the monastery and the Villa Julia; only a hard-trodden path up a slope of rock and scrub open to the sun. Beside the path a stream tumbled, bordered with ferns and flowers, white anemones and poppies. Most days Georgi would stable his new mount in the village or, boylike, leave it lying on the rocks at the foot of the track. Unless goats ate the tyres, it would be safe. The machine was Georgi's. No one on the island would touch it without invitation.

But today it must be taken home, to show to Mama.

Julia Marsden rarely went down to the village except on Sundays when, mounted on the high wooden saddle of her donkey and wearing a stiff black silk gown, she attended the Greek Orthodox church with her children, and afterwards drank a glass or two of wine under the awning of the *taverna* with her women friends and relations and listened to the family news. Twenty years ago Julia had been a village girl like the others, but even then, Evie sometimes thought, she must have had some special quality which set her apart. For it had been Julia the Englishman, George Marsden, wooed and married. For Julia he built the white villa up on the fertile little plateau, bought and cultivated the land which now supported his family.

And ever since her wedding day, Julia had set herself apart. Never failing to take an interest in island affairs, in the children and grandchildren, the weddings and funerals; but aloof, like a great lady, like a queen.

Even when George Marsden left her, tiring perhaps of seven years of village life and the cultivation of his

9

lemons, and longing for the company of educated men of his own kind, Julia never relaxed her dignity. George was merely taking a holiday, as he deserved. He would be back, in his own time.

The pair had to carry the bike up the last stretch, and emerged on to an open plateau like a ledge on the hillside. Here were fields carefully cultivated to grow fruit and vegetables. Julia's olive trees, and those belonging to the four old Brothers of the monastery, were separated by a wide ditch.

'There's Mama,' said Georgi. 'Working in the field. She said I needn't, because of my birthday, but I didn't want her to do my work. I'm a man now. I'm eleven and I can manage fine. When I'm bigger we'll be able to cultivate right up to the edge of the Brothers' land, and we'll be rich and you'll be able to get married.'

Evie hugged his narrow shoulders. 'I don't want to get married. I want to stay here, with you and Mama, for ever and ever. If I were a man, I think I'd go into a monastery and be a Brother, and live with God, and grow things.'

'And paint icons? I shan't. I shall plant grapefruit and oranges, and stop growing all these tiresome vegetables. I'll plant the whole island with my fruit trees, and sit and watch them grow money for me.'

'You won't. If Mama sells the house, you'll go to England to school, and get educated and be a business man in an office. That's what she wants.'

'It's *my* land. She can't sell it.'

'If it's for your own good, she can. Father wanted a proper English education for you. Everybody knows that. So they'll tell her she's right to carry out her husband's wishes.'

'If they force me to go, I shall run away.'

Evie was torn between her respect for her mother's

authority and sympathy with the boy. Lying awake on hot nights, she had formulated a dozen plans for circumventing her mother's determination, and comforted herself with the knowledge that there would never be enough money to send Georgi away, unless the house and land were sold. And who would buy? If any man on Exos had the price of it, he would have bought already, for the land was fertile and well cultivated, sheltered from winds and watered by the stream which rarely dried up even at the height of summer. The real danger lay in the homecomers; islanders returning with a fat bank balance after a few years' work in Greece, Malta, Rome, or even England, ready to invest it in land and olives to support them in old age.

Georgi, crimson with effort, pointed down to the village and the shimmering sea. 'There was a man in the caique, a foreigner. Perhaps he'll buy the house.'

The dazzling white houses were like toys now. The boats lay still, painted toys on painted water. The quay, the street, were deserted. For hours, the men would sit in the shade on those ubiquitous wooden chairs, playing cards, playing chess, talking, staring into nowhere. Even the stranger had gone.

Evie weighed up the possibilities, then shook her head. 'Too poor. He had no luggage, only a pack on his back. He hadn't a camera, or a gold wristwatch. He'll stay for a few days at the *taverna*, walk in the hills a bit, then he'll go away. Don't worry about him.'

Their mother had seen them, and waved. Georgi rode towards her, wobbling a little on the narrow trodden path towards the house.

'Mama,' Evie reproved. 'It's too hot to work outside. Come indoors and let me make coffee for you. Everyone is resting in the shade but my foolish mother.'

The rooms of the villa had high blue ceilings and arched windows, which were now shuttered for coolness. On the seaward side of the house, George Marsden had built a wide balcony with a trellised roof which over the years had become smothered with vines and jasmine. To this cool terrace, Evie brought the coffee.

Georgi lay on his stomach, entranced by the shining splendour of his present. He reached out an inattentive hand for the chilled bottle of his favourite fizzy drink, and applied the straw to his lips absent-mindedly.

'He is happy,' Julia murmured. She was tired, and despised herself for being so, after so little work today. It seemed no time at all since she had been a girl able to work long hours in the fields, or to shake down ripe olives all day, or help with the lemon harvest and dance on the quay till midnight afterwards.

'Do you think Georgi's father will be pleased with him?' she asked now, not for the first time. 'He's a fine boy for his age, isn't he? And clever, the Brothers tell me. Were there any letters for us, by the boat?'

'Nothing, Mama. Do you think—I mean, have you ever wondered if our father is still alive? All these years, and you still wait for a letter. Wouldn't we be happier if we accepted the idea that he will never come back?'

'*Never come back?* Of course your father will come back! He has a wandering nature, that's all. He loves us all, and he will want to see us soon. He'll be pleased with you, Evie. You take after him, with your fair hair and blue eyes. You look English.'

Evie bit her lip and kept silent. That she resembled her absent father annoyed her unspeakably. As the years stretched out, as she saw hope fade in her mother's eyes, as even small Georgi had to work to grow and harvest the lemons which supported them, the childish affection for her father had changed to implacable hatred. But her mother must never know it, so she merely nodded.

'But his son! I've failed him there. He wanted a

proper education for his boy, an English education. He will be grieved with me about that.'

'It wasn't your fault, Mama. Father should have come back, or sent you the money. Where would we get the fare to England, or clothes for the boy? And who would arrange it all for us? We don't know anybody over there.'

'When I sell the house—'

'Mama, give up this idea. Georgi is old enough to know what he wants, and we should respect his wishes. He has a good inheritance here, land and a fine house. What need is there to send him away from everything he knows, and everybody he loves, to that horrible country where it rains every day and is so cold? Will he thank you for it, when he becomes a man without roots, without the house and land his father bought? Do be careful what you're doing.'

Julia shot her daughter a look half defiant, half ashamed. Two passions fought in her, two deeply-rooted traditions; the passion of the peasant for land, and the ingrained belief that her husband was lord and master, to be obeyed even in his absence. To obey her husband's wishes would rob her son of his patch of fertile soil, but to disregard them was unthinkable. Already she had dilly-dallied so long. She sighed heavily.

'If only George would come, I should not have to decide. Evie, I think you must go and find him, tell him the boy is growing up.'

Evie sat back on her naked heels and stared at her mother. She felt cold with shock. How long had that idea been simmering in Mama's devious mind?

'But where should I find him, Mama? It could take years. He could be anywhere in the whole world. Where could I begin?'

13

'In England. There must be people who know him.'

Evie sighed impatiently. 'Mama, I've told you again and again, England is enormous, many times bigger than Cyprus. Nicosia is a village compared with London. There are millions of people, packed as close together as pebbles on a beach.'

'They must have some way of knowing whether a man is alive or dead, if they're so clever.'

'He might be in America, or Africa.'

Georgi had fallen asleep on the floor beside the bike. Now he woke up suddenly and asked if he might ride across to the monastery to show the Brothers. 'They'll be interested, Mama. Truly they will. And I can tell them about the boat, and who's home. And about the Englishman.'

Julia darted a look at Evie. 'What Englishman?'

'A stranger. He came on the boat. He hadn't any luggage, only a canvas bag. He looked English—well, not American.'

'Where is he now?'

Evie shrugged. 'How should I know? In the *taverna*, perhaps, or asleep under an olive tree. He's one of those holidaymakers who come with nothing and expect everything on the cheap. No one down there will make a fortune out of him, I'll be bound.'

'I have a fool for a daughter! Why didn't you invite him here? He might know something about your father. He might even have a message for us. Or—or he might have come to buy a house on Exos.'

'Mama, I tell you, he isn't rich. And a man doesn't buy a house without his wife. And if Father sent him with a message, he'd tell him where we lived. Dear, sweet little Mama, please stop hoping so much. I can't bear it when you're disappointed. The

14

world's so big, so many people in it. Yet you expect every stranger who lands here will know about George Marsden.'

Georgi jigged from one foot to the other. 'May I go, Mama?'

'Yes, yes, boy. But don't be a trouble to the Brothers. If they are busy, come home. And don't forget to say a prayer in the chapel before you leave.'

Georgi ran off happily.

'One day,' said his mother, folding her hands on her lap again, 'the Englishman will pass this way to visit the monastery. Visitors always do. I shall invite him in, to taste our honey and sheep cheese, and I shall ask him if he wants to buy the house.'

'A house? A tent, more like. He'll laugh at you.'

Julia drew herself up. 'Nobody laughs at *me*, Evie, least of all, a guest in my house. Where is this man staying? At the *taverna*? When I was a girl it was famous for its fleas. Your father stayed there two nights when he arrived; and took his bed into the fields, until my mother offered him our hospitality.'

'Funny, to think my existence depends upon a flea. If they'd bitten harder, he might have left the island after one night. If they hadn't bitten at all, he'd have remained at the *taverna* and you'd never have married him.'

'Yes, I should. He fell in love with me the moment he landed. We girls were watching the boat arriving at the quay, and laughing, the way girls do. He looked up and saw us, five of us. There and then, he fell in love with the girl in the middle. I had a sky-blue silk dress, and white lace round the neck of my dress. It looked so pretty, he said, against my brown skin. You never make lace, Evie. We all used to be so proud to wear the lace we'd made ourselves.'

'I'm not a lace person. I wish I'd been a boy.

Anyway, I can wear your lace when I have to. You made enough for a whole family, and it's far more beautiful than anything I could manage.'

'You're like your father, you have no patience to sit still. Bring me my embroidery. You are right, it's too hot now to work outside.'

Like most of the Exos women, Julia earned a little by her exquisite embroidery on linen, which was collected once a year and sent over to Cyprus to be sold in the luxury hotels of Nicosia. She was now engaged upon a circular white tablecloth, covered so closely with openwork that hardly an inch of the original material remained visible. Already she had worked on it for almost two years, and this summer she hoped to finish it. It would find a buyer among the rich Americans, and the high price paid for it would scarcely repay Julia for the hundreds of hours she had spent on it.

Evie settled her mother to work in a spot where the sun would not reach too soon, with all her materials round her; then she changed into a sleek black bathing suit and ran to bathe. There was a short cut to the best beach down the side of the seaward-facing cliff, down which she scrambled, dropping from one herb-scented ledge to another till she reached the level patch of ground where flowers grew in profusion; anemones, marigolds, daisies, cyclamen, wild gladioli, and lilies. The air was awash with scent and loud with honey bees.

Only a small cypress grove now, between Evie and the water, which shimmered in the sun in bars of emerald and azure. Eager for the pleasure of the salt water, she ran, head thrown back and fair hair streaming.

Till she fell headlong and landed heavily across the chest and arms of a stranger sleeping under a pepper tree.

His voice spoke in her ear. Very loud and startled it was, and with an accent the like of which she had never heard. The grip of his arms was like iron.

'Glory be! I'm sleeping under a pepper tree dreaming of angels when the goddess Aphrodite herself falls spang out of the sky into me arms. And she screaming blue murder! For the love of holy Michael, woman, will you shut up yelling!'

Evie, the breath knocked out of her, stopped struggling and sat up, first removing herself from the man's bare chest.

'Why don't you keep your legs to yourself?' she demanded crossly when she could speak. 'I didn't see you, stretched out flat among the tree shadows. Lucky I didn't break a limb, falling like that.'

'I did my best to catch you,' he said, not humbly. 'Why don't you look where you're going so fast?'

'There's never anyone here. You're the Englishman who landed this morning, aren't you? Do you have fleas?'

'Good lord, no. Why? It's not a question I'd ask my best friend, never mind a total stranger.'

'I mean, at the *taverna*, if you're staying there. I didn't mean to ask out loud, but we were talking of it, my mother and I, and the question of fleas turned out to be quite important to my existence. Sorry, it sort of popped out. I don't suppose you have.'

'If I find one in the *taverna*'s bed, I'll let you know at once,' he promised gravely. 'My name, since you didn't ask, is Rory McDermot, and I'm not English.'

'Good. I dislike the English intensely.'

'So do I. Let us sit down here where it's cool, and explain to each other why we have no use for the English.'

'My father is one. But it's not on account of him, exactly. What about you?'

17

'It's because I come from Ireland.'

'Ireland? Where's that? What is it famous for?'

'For princesses, ma'am. We export them. Have you never heard of the Princess Etain?'

'Never. What do you mean, export them?'

'In men's hearts, ma'am. Not an Irishman the width of the world but has a princess, maybe two, in his heart.'

She saw at once that this was no Englishman, but a man who could tell a stranger a legend at the drop of a hat. She fell in with his mood at once.

'So the world must be full of your princesses. Do they never get home again?'

'Oh yes, now and again. Sometimes a princess will fall right out of the sky into a man's arms, same like now. You were going swimming?'

She was sufficiently collected to see now that he, too, was wearing swimming things, and was a great deal browner and leaner than the average holidaymaker who landed on Exos. His straight fair hair was sun-bleached, his jaw and nose aggressive, his eyes blue and bright as washed pebbles. For the first time in her life, masculinity—the simple fact that here was a young, personable man—intrigued her.

He smelt good. She wrinkled her nose, so recently squashed against his bare chest; thinking that he smelt more like the young freshness of her brother than like any man of the village. They smelt, mostly, of goat and sweat, fish, garlic and cheese.

Out of nowhere, fear dropped a shadow across her mind. This was how it had been with her mother. A blond god out of the blue, and love blossoming suddenly; and a lifetime of waiting and watching for that wandering god to come again. How it had always been, perhaps, for the girls of the islands, right back to the time when, they say, gods walked the earth like men.

18

She retreated from the situation. 'Yes, I—I always swim alone. And I don't like to be watched.'

'Point taken.' He unwound himself, in one smooth movement coming to his feet. 'I'll go. I'm sorry, I never asked if you were hurt. You did go a purler.'

She frowned. 'Purler? I don't know that word.'

'A bump. That's one your father didn't teach you. I suppose you speak fluent Greek too?'

'My mother is Greek—Exos Greek.'

'I see. And you live here? Up on the cliff? Isn't that where the monastery is? I must walk up there and have a look at it. They say the Brothers paint magnificent icons.'

If he went to the monastery, he would pass the Villa Julia and Mama would invite him in, and sell him the house whether he wanted it or not. 'No,' she said quickly. 'I mean, they do paint, but it's rubbish really. Nothing up there is worth the climb. The best part of the island is to the north and west. Go there. You'll like it.'

She turned and ran, fear giving her feet wings across the white sand.

I'm not afraid of him, she thought. He's kind and gentle, and tells fairy stories. What I'm afraid of is myself.

She met the warm, silky water with a quiver of pure pleasure, rested upon it and swam strongly and steadily. After a time, she turned on her back and floated, looking back towards the land. From here one could see the white monastery with its little bell tower; and the pink-washed walls of the Villa Julia.

Also the cypress grove, which would be empty now.

The water had washed away her foolish panic and quietened her beating heart. She trod water, regretfully. It would have been pleasant, after all, to have company for her swim. He would swim well, she fancied, with those strong brown arms cleaving the blue and emerald.

We export princesses—and sometimes one falls out of the sky.

She laughed and dived, swimming underwater with eyes open, seeing small bright fish flash and turn as one; shells on the sea floor, and coralline weed.

Well, he would soon tire of the island north and west. There was nothing to see there but a small coppermine, and a flat grey saltbed. The stranger would be back.

CHAPTER TWO

FOR two days Evie kept a careful watch for the Irishman, worked in the field close to home, in the house, or even, desperately, at her somewhat lumpy embroidery on the shaded balcony. But Rory McDermot did not approach, either from the seaward side of the cliff, nor from the village up the track by the tumbling little river.

She had no idea what she intended to do if he did appear. Head him off, if possible, or steer him wide of the house in the monastery direction so that her mother should not see him.

For three years now, Julia Marsden had been talking vaguely of selling the house up on the cliff, which was too big for three, and settling down in the village among her cronies in a small cottage belonging to her own family, which stood empty because too many cousins and second cousins were leaving the island these days, to make their fortunes in a bigger sphere. Some actually did, but showed no inclination to return to Exos to a tiny, cramped house with an outside stair and no sanitation. But now, startled by the impact of Georgi's eleventh birthday, she meant business. Evie could feel the change, in her bones.

It was, the girl reflected as she hoed along the neat rows of vegetables, a thousand pities that the Villa Julia was Julia's. By one of those extraordinary quirks of the English character so incomprehensible to the islanders, George Marsden had bought the place, not for himself but for his wife. There was nothing to stop her selling if she wished. And Julia could be so gently determined to get her own way that she was capable of selling it to the Irishman even if all he wanted was a melon or a ripe pomegranate. The only safe way was to keep the two apart.

But on the third day Evie became bored with keeping so close to home, and longed for a chat with Sofia, who was sure to know what the man was up to. Sofia was very reliable with news, for she was related to the Stratos family who kept the *taverna*, and, when it suited her, put in an hour or two as waitress. Small as the tourist trade was for Exos, Sofia liked to be at the centre of it. Besides, she said, it was good practice. One day she'd be off, to see the world of Cyprus or even further afield, and it is good to have a trade in one's hands then.

Sofia laughed, throwing her head back and showing her strong creamy throat. She had a new black dress on, and a strip of lace, and a scarlet silk apron which last year she had worn only for feast days.

'He's mad, that Irishman. This morning at dawn he hired a donkey and rode off to the coppermines. Would you believe it? He says everyone in his country rides a donkey, but they don't have wooden saddles like ours. He took some food in a bag. What, for goodness' sake, is there to see in a coppermine?'

'Perhaps he's a miner? Perhaps he wants to buy copper.'

'Not he. He has no money. You should see his bedroom. Only two shirts, Evie! He's twenty-six and not married, and his eyes are grey.'

Evie opened her mouth to say *blue*, but asked instead how Sofia knew.

'From his passport, of course. He left it on the wooden chest.'

'You can't read English. If it *is* in English?'

'Your young brother can. I brought it down in my pocket and asked him yesterday.'

'Sofia! You know it was wrong. You shouldn't spy on a guest. Nor should Georgi.'

The plump shoulders shrugged. 'He isn't my guest. Why are you so interested? You haven't asked about Marcus.'

Evie frowned, puzzled. 'Marcus?'

'He came home the day the stranger came. I told you.'

'Why should I ask about him? He was always a horrid creature. We agreed we didn't like him, even before he went away.'

Sofia slapped her arm and giggled. 'Do grow up, Evie! Marcus has changed. He's charming now. Such beautiful manners, and he's grown really handsome. You'd hardly know him, if you're still thinking of that tiresome, spotty youth we used to know. He's a man of the world, no less. He has money, too; and a very good job in Athens. You should have been here last night. Nothing would please him but dancing on the quay, with the lanterns out, and everything. We're going to do it again tonight. Will your mother let you come?'

'She might. I'd have to bring Georgi. He wouldn't want to miss anything. Does the Irishman dance?'

Sofia nodded vigorously. 'And plays the accordion too. And once he sang. It was a terribly sad song, I think. Everybody went quiet while he sang it. Music over the water can be sad, don't you think?'

Evie made up her mind. 'I'll come.'

'That's right. And wear your white dress. Don't come in that old black one, though you're perfectly capable of such a trick. Put your hair up in a loop on top of your head, and wear shoes and stockings. Honestly, Evie, anyone would think you about fifteen, not a lady of eighteen turned. You're so skinny too.'

'I know. I wish I were as plump as you, and with your colouring.' Evie sighed regretfully, aware that in

23

the white dress she looked even paler and more insignificant than Sofia. But she had no other, and had never bothered to take the boat as far as Kyrenia to fit herself out with something more fashionable.

Princesses, he'd said. Girls with bouncing black hair and bright brown eyes, and lips like the inside of a ripe pomegranate bursting on the tree.

She finished her shopping and began the walk home with a laden basket on each arm. Her feet felt light as air, and even going up the steepest part of the climb she seemed to be skimming over the ground, uplifted by excited anticipation. In some book, she remembered, there had been flaxen-haired princesses, and it may be the Irishman thought as much of long straight fair hair as of short bouncy curls that shone like black olives.

In the white dress, with shoes and stockings and her hair piled high and tied with a broad blue ribbon that matched her eyes, an evening of dancing under the lanterns on the waterfront might be exciting. Music, and the coloured lights dancing in long bars across the water, and maybe the Irishman would sing his sad song again.

She thought a little about Marcus. Could that rough, detestable boy really have become a good-looking man with beautiful manners, as Sofia said? The warm dark hours after sunset promised to be interesting, and she hugged her heavy baskets to her, hardly able to contain her delight. Such a perfect day! Such a wonderful place to live! How could anyone bear to leave it?

In the late afternoon Rory McDermot trudged along a hot dusty road, leading a reluctant donkey. He was angry. He enlivened his walk by rehearsing what he meant to say to that lying little creature who had sent him off on a wild goose chase to the other side of the island, to find nothing for his trouble but the ugly waste tips of an old coppermine and the grey concrete huts of the mine offices and workers' dwellings.

It was longer than he had thought since his donkey-riding days in Connemara. In those days he had been able to kick the hairy ribs of his mount with his bare heels, but now his feet almost reached the ground. Then, he had ridden bareback; today he was lumbered with a high wooden saddle directly descended, it seemed, from some medieval instrument of torture. If some horny-handed man—such as her father—put her across his knee and walloped her till she couldn't sit down, it would be no more than she deserved. Too late for him to do it, more's the pity. The child was almost a woman, very nearly a beauty.

Suddenly he remembered his talk of princesses, and laughed aloud, startling the delicate-legged chocolate-coloured donkey. Much talk of their beauty, pale faces, golden hair and such. Nothing to say the same princesses of old time mightn't be the great fibbers.

The sea came into view around a bend in the road, and the row of date palms along the waterfront of the village. He jerked the halter, and mounted the donkey again, groaning at his protesting muscles.

'Come on, Beelzebub, get moving! Let us ride in like a pair of conquerors. At least you'll tell no one I've walked as far as you have today, for the sake of your thin legs as much as for my creaking bones. I've gone soft, boyo. I've seen the time when I thought nothing to see a grown man riding a donkey carrying two loaded panniers of peat besides.'

The donkey, smelling home, put on a show of willingness and Rory had to watch out for his dangling feet on the rough road. He had no wish to break an ankle, dashing it against a boulder.

If there was dancing again tonight, he would cut a poor figure, stiff as he was. Last night he had had plenty of choice of partners, and the plump little Sofia had used him to tease the handsome Greek boy, Marcus. Well, he didn't mind helping in a good cause, and twice he remembered snatching the girl almost out of the Greek's grasp. Between whiles he'd looked around once or twice hoping to see his companion of the afternoon, young Aphrodite fallen out of the sky knocking the breath out of him; but she wasn't there. Too young, perhaps, and kept close at home by strict parents.

One day soon, he thought, flicking the donkey with a cut stick, we shall meet again, my girl, and I shall give you the rough edge of my tongue, for liars I cannot abide.

A lizard, startled by his rumbling voice, flicked off a grey boulder and vanished. The donkey pricked his ears and broke into a trot. It could not understand the English words but knew from experience how a man's voice sounded when he was angry.

Evie washed her white dress and while waiting for it to be ironing-dry, corrected Georgi's arithmetic.

'Look, little one, if you get your sums wrong now, it doesn't matter so much. But you must try to get them right, because when you're a man, a grower, with big groves of lemons, grapefruit, olives, it will matter then. If you get your sums wrong, a whole year's work could be wasted. You'll have to buy and sell, pay wages and know how many trees to plant in an acre of land. You'll have to ship your crops to the mainland and pay freight at so much a load.'

'When I'm the boss, I'll make somebody else do the sums.'

'Then you'll be cheated.'

His mouth firmed. He looked up scowling, his strong brows drawn together. 'No one will cheat *me*.'

'Not if you're cleverer than they are. That's why I make you have extra lessons, little one. I know it comes hard, in the heat and when there are so many better things to do.' She sat cross-legged on the floor beside him. 'Look now. Let's start again. Pretend you're the owner of a simply enormous plantation and I've come to buy half your crop.'

His serious eyes met hers. 'Evie, Mama will send me away if she sells the house. Don't let her. I just want to stay here, on my island, and grow things. If I have to go away to the cold and dark, I'll die. I *know* I'll die.'

She swept him into her arms. 'I'll try. I swear I'll try my best to keep you here. But you'll have to help yourself too. You'll have to work at getting an education here, or the priest will tell Mama you're to go away to learn more. We all want what's best for you, Georgi. Only Mama's idea of what is best is to do what Father would have wanted for you, and she might be right.'

The boy twisted out of her arms and flung himself on the floor sobbing. 'Don't let her make me go! I want to stay here, at home. I don't want her to sell the house to get the money. It's mine. The land is mine. If she sells it, I'll never get it back. It isn't fair, Evie!'

That was the rub. What *was* fair, for the child? Was it right to keep an intelligent boy here on the island, taught only by the priest and a girl? Would he later be as full of reproaches as now he was full of pleading? He had an English father, alive or dead. Ought he not to see something of England, then?

But could it be right to sell the boy's inheritance of good land and good house? To send him, protesting, away to a future he might not care for?

She crouched down beside him, stroked his hair. 'I won't let her sell this land, Georgi, that I swear. Even if you do have to go away to be taught, you'll have the land to come back to, if you choose. I'll do anything— absolutely anything at all—to keep your land for you. The house I may not be able to save, if Mama is set on it; but we shall have a house down in the village, the one that belonged to Mama's family, and it's not a bad house, is it?'

'It's not *my* house.'

'No. I'll fight any idea of selling this house, too, but I may not win. We might have to compromise, Georgi, but there are two of us, and only one of Mama, so we shan't lose all the battles.'

Georgi dried his eyes, but he was too upset for further arithmetic, so Evie sent him off to play while she ironed her dress. 'Then we'll go swimming, I promise.'

The white dress had been new for Easter Sunday last year. Evie pressed the lace around the neck carefully; she would wear the Maltese cross on a gold chain which her father had given her all those years ago. She remembered so little of him, but she did recall the day he had come home with the little trinket in his pocket, and Mama had made her put it away till she was older.

I'm older now, she decided firmly. I shall wear the necklet now, every day if I want to.

The ironing finished, she experimented with her hair. Easy enough to plait it into a single heavy rope, but not so easy to twist it into a coil and pin it high on her head. But the result pleased her. She touched her neck wonderingly. Now, it did seem to matter that it was longer and thinner than Sofia's. Under the coronet of hair, her small head was poised gracefully, reminding her of one of the old Greek statues in the museum she had visited once as a schoolgirl. Like the head on a coin!

Shaking with excitement, she tugged off the old

28

black dress and carefully dropped the white one over her head without damaging the coronet. If the piled-up hair could work a tiny miracle for her head and neck, perhaps it would work for the dress too.

Looking at herself in the long glass, she fell from joy to depression. The dress would not do. It was a school-girl's Sunday dress, neat but shapeless. And she had grown out of it. It wouldn't even fasten properly. Dismay shook her, a lump rose in her throat. After the long hours of happy anticipation, she would not consider running down to the village in her black dress, with her hair swinging over her shoulders. Yesterday, she could have done it. But yesterday existed in time past. Today was different because she was different.

She ran out on to the terrace, where Julia was embroidering in the cool shade.

'Mama! My dress!'

Julia looked up, and kept on looking in silence for a long-drawn-out minute. Then she stabbed her needle into her work and stood up.

'No, Evie, it won't do. You can't go in that. We must do something about it.'

'Moving the buttons again won't do. It's a child's dress.'

Julia, surprisingly, kissed her daughter lightly. She was a reserved woman, not demonstrative ever. 'And you are not a child any more! How time races away. Your father should see you now, Evie. You are going to be beautiful very soon. He always said you had a perfect nose and the rest of your face would live up to it eventually. Come along, I'll find something for you to wear. And I think I must come too. I can't let you run wild any more.'

The idea of having a chaperone did not disconcert Evie in the least. All the mothers would be there, sitting in rows behind the little tables, each with her glass of wine, her gossip, her son or daughter to be proud of; to be the only dancer who had no mama or papa watching would be odd and uncomfortable. What did worry her was the fear of what Mama might produce as suitable for her to wear.

There was a great carved chest in Mama's bedroom, built of oak bleached and stained with sea water. Her father insisted that it was British and had come with the Crusaders, perhaps floated ashore from some shipwreck all those centuries ago. This Julia now unlocked, though it took both of them to lift back the lid.

The first layer was graveclothes for all the family, handwoven, bleached, and ironed ready. Next came several suits belonging to George Marsden, smelling strongly of cloves and put by for his son if George himself never came back. Then there was the family wedding dress, the lace a trifle yellowed now, the tiny crown wrapped in white linen.

'Time we were thinking about a husband for you, Evie. Your father wouldn't want you to marry an island man. He'll come and take you to England, you'll see. You'll live in London and have a proper house with taps indoors and a chain to pull, and what your father called a proper lavatory seat. Some of them even have taps in the bedroom.'

'I know. But they don't have the sun, or the sea. When I open my shutters in the morning, the sun comes in like a sword, a long bright sword lying across the floor.'

'And a washing machine.'

'I'll need it,' the girl said glumly. 'Everything covered in black soot, and raining every single day so you can't dry anything.'

Julia sat back on her heels and looked up at her daughter quizzically. 'Sometimes I think you exaggerate when you talk about England, child. I'm sure your father wouldn't stay there so long if it rained every single day. He loved—loves—the sun, too. As you do.'

'Then why doesn't he come home? Isn't there anything else in the chest? I can't wear the wedding dress tonight.'

'Be patient.' Carefully, with some grunting and groaning, Julia leaned far into the deep oak, and brought up a wrapped package. 'It's what I wore for feast days. There can't be many about now. Open it, child.'

A cornflower-blue satin skirt over layers of white starched petticoats. A yellow bibbed apron embroidered in purple and black, green and blue and crimson. A white blouse with full sleeves tight at the wrist, a pretty lace cap. To wear with it, long white stockings and scarlet shoes.

'Oh, Mama!' Evie breathed. 'Is it really for me?'

'I don't see why not. I had it from my mother. Will it fit? I had a better figure than you—round as a cherry, I was. It's the English in you that makes you so skinny.'

News of the previous night's dancing having spread on the wind, the village of Peleas was full when Julia arrived, stately in black satin and sitting very erect on her donkey. Georgi led the animal, and Evie, self-conscious and shy but trying hard not to show it, followed in the blue swinging skirt over a dozen freshly pressed petticoats.

Straw mats had been thrown over the wooden stands which had been empty all winter, and tables set up under their shade. Coloured electric lights swung from end to end of the quay, bright painted chairs were set out, and the mixed bag of musicians were already in place in one of the fishing boats. Families from the small Turkish village on the other side of the island had walked over and were greeted as friends, the cruel passions of the Cyprus feud of no concern to neighbours who had lived cheek by jowl for generations. The men came in their black baggy trousers, the women with black shawls over their heads, out of which their oval faces peered, smiling. The proprietor of the *taverna* dusted off the communal hubble-bubble pipe and set it on the table outside to be smoked by three men at once.

Julia found a seat and held court. Half the people present were related to her, more or less distantly, and came to pay their respects. Soon she had a handful of flowers, and a bloom tucked into her hair.

Sofia was spellbound by Evie's dress. 'I can't wait to show Marcus! He'll be so surprised. He used to pull your hair.'

Evie grinned. 'I pulled his. If he tries it again, so will I. Is—er—anybody else here?'

Sofia's laugh made heads turn in their direction. 'You silly! Everybody's here! There are to be fireworks. Marcus brought them, great boxes! If you mean the Irishman, I think he's gone to bed. Not that he'll sleep in this uproar.'

Evie knew a stab of disappointment. Her own appearance in Julia's long looking-glass had startled her into the realisation that she possessed a special quality of looks which might well compete with the other girls of the island; even with Sofia, who, up till now, had been Evie's ideal. Clad in her heavenly-blue dress, the lace cap on her silvery-blonde hair, cheeks flushed a little with excitement, she had stared and stared, unable to believe her eyes.

With her hands she had explored the soft curves of her figure, understanding that there might be a more subtle beauty than the emphasised plumpness of her friends. Skinny, they called her teasingly. But out of

32

the shapeless old black frock she wasn't skinny at all. She was—

'Beautiful?' she whispered. 'Am I? Could someone think me beautiful, I wonder?'

She was trembling with the sudden discovery of herself. All the way down to the village, she had hugged the knowledge. No one would notice, of course. She would still be the pale, skinny one, among the dark plump beauties. But perhaps Rory, the Irishman, might see—he with his talk of princesses. She held her head high as if it bore an imaginary crown.

And now the wretched man had gone to bed. As if the dancing didn't matter, as if he despised them all, the laughing girls, the friendly hospitality, the music, the fireworks to come.

'We're not good enough for him, then?' she said to Sofia. 'Well, we don't want strangers here. Once tourists come, all the fun will be for them, and we'll only exist for cooking and serving meals. Come on, let's find Marcus.'

Marcus had found them. He came towards them smiling, a bunch of spring flowers in his hands. He had filled out in his two years' absence. He was, Evie thought, two inches taller. As Sofia had said, he was a man, and good to look at.

His dark eyes were shining with the happiness of being home, being king of the castle tonight as provider of the fireworks to come. The girl he chose would be queen tonight. Of old, unwritten custom, he would make his choice with the flowers he had picked and tied into a bunch with ribbon. If it was not exactly a proposal of marriage, the presentation of the flowers was certainly an indication of a strong interest in the recipient; the opening gambit in a courtship to come.

And Marcus was making straight for Sofia. Evie glanced quickly at her friend, feeling a faint chill of sadness. She would miss Sofia, for with instinctive prescience she knew that the long island courtship, and marriage, would put an end to the closeness. Friends they would always be, but after tonight, perhaps, never so warm and near to each other.

Sofia's face was easy to read, for one who knew her—proud, happy, shy. Not yet in love but standing tiptoe on the edge of it.

Marcus walked straight past her and put the flowers into Evie's hands. Then he kissed her firmly on both cheeks.

'No, Marcus. No!' She pushed away, trying to make him take back the bouquet. The heady scent of it choked her.

'Come on, Evie!' He laughed happily. 'Don't pretend you've never been kissed before.' He took a pace back and looked her up and down. 'You've grown up in two years. Where's that tomboy scarecrow gone? You're the prettiest girl here, and I'm claiming the right to the first dance.'

Sick at heart, she asked, 'Don't you want to dance with Sofia?'

'Sure I do. With every girl there is. But you first, because you're the prettiest.'

No one, as far as she knew, had ever refused a young man's flowers. It would be an insult to him and his family. It might start a feud that lasted for a century. She cast a helpless glance at Sofia, whose smile was stuck to her mouth like a left-over flower on a winter tree. Then Marcus whirled her off into the dancing.

'What a surprise for a man to come home and find all the girls so pretty!'

'What a surprise,' she returned, 'to find you so tall and handsome.' And so stupid, she added to herself. 'Aren't they much prettier in Athens?'

'Some are. But they don't smell of honey and flowers,

34

and most of them judge a man by the depth of his pocket. I like kissing them, but I'd never feel like marrying one.'

'Cheers for the island, then. Are you staying long?'

'That depends.' He smiled down at her, and increased the pressure of his arm around her.

'You don't want to come home and settle down?'

'Not yet. In time I might. I'd like my own restaurant, but on one of the bigger islands.'

'That takes money, Marcus.'

He shrugged. 'It can be earned. With the right wife, it wouldn't take so long. Two can earn and save quicker than one.'

'Two of the same mind. You'd have to pick the right one.'

He laughed. 'I know what I want, Evie. There's time enough, and we're young yet.'

We?

With relief she saw a way to withdraw without offence. 'There's Melanie. She's brought her baby. I *must* see it. It's her first. Doesn't she look proud?'

With a quick wriggle she was out of his grasp and among the baby-worshippers gathered round the young mother. She prayed hard to St. Polystemon to make Marcus go back to Sophia. It didn't seem the sort of prayer to bother the greater saints with, but St. Poly had been a boy of the island himself, so they said; and not more than twenty years old when he died for his faith. So perhaps he would understand how it was to be young and in love, and hoping too much.

Father Bernard, the island priest, smiled and patted the chair beside him. His squat black-clad figure was never far away from the centre of any activity—except swimming. Every child firmly believed that Father Bernard had been born into his long black gown, with his tall, veiled headdress stuck on his head, though they

35

were prepared to believe there might have been a time when his beard was not so long, so curly, or so grey.

'Marcus has become a fine man,' the priest commented, his eyes everywhere and smiling on his beloved flock. 'I hope to see him married to one of our own, an island girl.'

'You will, Father. I'm sure of it.'

'Yes, I've noticed a man comes back to his own, if he has good sense. I like to think of our dear St. Poly as a lad like Marcus, a big handsome boy.'

'Do you think he pulled the girls' hair and tormented them?'

The priest shook with quiet laughter. 'I'm sure he did. I know I did, when I was his age. But it didn't come to me to become a martyr, you see. Bless me, I remember your mother in that dress, Evie. It is the same one? It was the day your father arrived, so he probably set eyes on her for the first time, wearing that very outfit. No wonder he loved her. And now it's your turn, eh?'

'Not yet. I have things to do. What's to become of Georgi, Father? My mother wants to sell the property to buy him a good education, but I don't think she should. It's his inheritance. A man with land, that's something.'

'An education is also something, child.'

'You teach him. I teach him. What can he learn that will be better for him? Where would it take him, all this education?'

'No one can say what a boy will become, Evie. I know this problem. Your mother has talked of it, many times. It is your father's wish. I think she should do it.'

'Against the boy's wish? Surely he has some rights? The right not to have his land sold over his head? Father, I think my father must be dead. If only I could be sure, one way or the other. How can one find out?'

'From official records, maybe. But where? There are British officials in Kyrenia, I believe. Certainly in Nicosia. Why don't you ask them?'

'I will. We must know soon, or it will be too late for Georgi. My mother is so determined. Sometimes I wonder if—' she hesitated, half afraid of seeming to criticise—'if she is too lonely up there, and wanting to come down to the house in the village among her friends. There'd be enough for her to live on, she says. She works on our land and I think she finds it hard going now.'

'You mean she is not altogether thinking of Georgi, but just a little of herself?'

Evie placed an impulsive hand on the priest's sleeve. 'Not consciously. If she's doing that, she's not aware of it. But you do understand I have to do what's best for Georgi? And I don't know what *is* best.'

The old man nodded two or three times. 'I, too, child. I have asked myself this question. Is your father dead or alive? If alive, his wishes must prevail. But if he is dead? Yes, I think you must try to find out.'

They were interrupted. An Irish voice said, 'Excuse me, Father. I would like a minute's private talk with this young lady.'

Evie turned quickly. Her heart thudded. It was Rory, and he had sought her out after all. She was suddenly self-conscious; aware of herself, her hands, her feet, the coiled hair on top of her head. The blood pounded in her long throat. In all the world there was only herself, and Rory the Irishman. The priest, Melanie and the baby, even Marcus and Sofia, did not exist.

'Come on,' he said roughly. 'I want you.'

She rose and followed him. He led her to a corner of

the harbour wall which was away from the crowd and deserted.

'Well,' he said in a cold, furious voice. 'Aren't you the splendid liar! A deceitful woman I cannot abide and never could. But I'll thank you to explain what was in the back of your mind, to be sending me and a harmless poor donkey on a wild goose chase which led nowhere but to a nasty old coppermine? Come on, you must have some reason.'

She swallowed. 'I thought you were interested in old things. The coppermine was started by the Romans.'

'Come off it, you little fool! I'm not swallowing that.' He gripped her arm above the elbow. 'I thought we were so friendly, but maybe I was wrong.' He spoke to her lightly. 'Coppermines, I said. I'm waiting?'

She could find no words, and kept silent.

'Look,' he said more gently, 'I was angry. In fact I spent several walking miles thinking how I'd like to spank you till you yelled. But I'm over that now, and just darned curious. You haven't the look of a liar, and I've met a few that had. What made you do it? What is there up by the monastery you don't want me to see?'

'Our house. It's for sale. I don't want anybody to buy it.'

'You flatter me. Do I have a moneyed appearance or something?'

'No. But my mother could sell you the moon, if she had a mind.'

His head went back as he laughed. 'I must meet her. She sounds as plausible as her daughter. But listen to me—' He shook a long finger close to her nose. 'If you ever tell me a whopping great fib again, or deceive me, so help me I'll—I'll tan the hide off you. Understand?'

'Don't try. The island men would kill you if you touched me.'

He nodded. 'They'd be right at that. But I'll give you the rough edge of my tongue, that I do promise. Now—about this house. How did you know I wanted to buy one? I didn't tell anybody.'

'I didn't know. It's just that ours could be for sale.'

'And you don't approve? But your parents must have a good reason. Have you considered they might need the money?'

'I have. The money is needed.'

'Then isn't your attitude extremely selfish? I don't think I can allow unreasonable prejudice to stand between me and a house I'd like to own. I give you fair warning, I intend to see your father about it tomorrow.'

'You can't. He's away.'

'Another of your lies?'

'No.'

He eyed her. 'That has a ring of truth. So your da is away. When is he expected home?'

She said firmly, 'My mother expects him home any day now.'

Their eyes met. She held his in a long stare. She was telling the truth—the precise truth, and had no reason for looking away.

'Any day?'

She nodded.

'Very well, then. I'll wait.'

Her mouth curved in a soft smile. 'Do just that, Irishman. Wait for my father.'

The first firework went up with a swoosh, and exploded red and green and gold.

CHAPTER THREE

THERE is nothing one can do about fireworks except stand and stare into the sky. Blue and silver, white and gold, scarlet and orange, there they go like pieces of magic, to the accompaniment of *Ahs* and *Ohs* from the throats of the enchanted.

Rory watched Evie's upturned face and his conscience smote him. Glory be, what had he done! This was no child, but a woman as lovely as any of his dreams. How could he have thought otherwise? A firm little chin, a tender mouth, the curve of a cheek so enchanting that—he went suddenly hot, his shirt stuck clammily to his back. What had he suggested? That he should spank her, no less. Called her a liar to her face.

Well, she *was* a liar, his aching bones reminded him sharply. As dishonest a deceiver as ever he'd met. And selfish, for if her mam and da needed the money from selling the house and she was going around telling lies to stop it being sold, she deserved all he'd said and more.

'Look here—' he began, half meaning to apologise in spite of himself.

She turned on him a look of cool disdain more snubbing than any words. Then, without a word, she ran to join the crowd watching the fireworks and melted into it. Not before he had observed her scarlet shoes, and ankles as delicate as a racing filly's, that a man might hold between finger and thumb. Too many girls, he reflected out of long experience, failed at the ankles.

He sat on the wall, shoulders hunched, and kicked himself in his mind for a clumsy, ham-handed lout. Women! Yesterday a child, a tomboy aping the dignity of a grown-up sister. Today, this.

Rory, my son, he reminded himself, you are finished with the female sex for ever. After Clodagh—no more. You will not put yourself in the power of a woman again. Be damned to the creatures—there are other things in this world to hold a man's interest and engage his soul.

Such as the house by the monastery. Tomorrow, if the blister on his heel permitted, he would take a walk up there and look at it. Again he felt the itch of excitement he had known on first seeing the island. This might be the place.

He had dreamed his dream ever since the day Clodagh rode away on the great bay horse paid for by the Englishman out of Somerset and was lost to him for ever. Young Clodagh he had grown up with and never thought but to marry. All that was water under the bridge now, and only the dream remained.

A white house on a cliff over a warm blue sea. A terrace shaded by vines. A high cool room of his own, in which to write and think, with only the bell of a monastery to mark the hours.

He did not find it odd that there was a monastery close to this house which might or might not be for sale. Wasn't there a monastery—or two, or three—on every island in the Mediterranean?

He would not be lonely in his house, for he planned to fill it with people with a need for solitude, silence and simplicity. A sort of monastic guest house, where the guests paid for necessities but no luxuries, if you didn't count simplicity as a luxury. A woman or two he would employ to clean and cook, though the guests must do their share.

There would be fruit sun-warm from the tree, milk from one's own goats, newlaid eggs, and bread fresh baked in a beehive-shaped abode oven in the yard.

Women? He had not decided. They could be a disturbing influence and he did not want his dream spoiled by emotions and strife. On the other hand, if there came one who genuinely needed his peace, for work or to mend her soul, the doors would not be closed, ever.

'*Kyrie*,' murmured Sofia at his side. 'You are not dancing?'

'Two blisters on my heels, and my bones aching from that terrible saddle?'

Sofia pouted, her lips soft and warm. 'Please, *kyrie*, dance with me. Just a few minutes. It's important to me.' She flicked a glance across the square to where Marcus was laughing with a group of boys. Her eyes were moist. Rory thought she had been crying and took pity on her.

'Very well, but be merciful. You're pretty enough to make dead bones jingle, and I'm not dead yet.'

He had observed the by-play with the flowers, and half blamed Evie for it. Sofia had been helpful from the moment he landed on Exos. She knew how to please a man in small ways and see to his comfort, and was also well aware of her own charming femininity. So if it would please this jolly little creature to be whirled under that Greek oaf's nose in the arms of a stranger, whirled she would be if it killed him.

As they moved out under the flickering lanterns, he caught sight of Evie sitting demurely in the circle of mothers. She looked somehow woebegone in spite of her magnificent dress; a child dressed up and nowhere to go. He reproached himself for not having asked her to dance, and chuckled suddenly, enjoying the trick she had played on him to keep him away from her part of the island.

Sofia looked up under her long dark lashes. 'The *kyrios* is amused?'

'Small donkey, large saddle—neither being my size. It must have looked funny, Sofia. You were kind enough not to laugh.'

She giggled. 'Your l-legs are so long, and the donkey's so short—'

Evie, watching covertly, saw them laughing heartily together. Are they laughing at me? she wondered miserably.

She felt small and guilty. Never before had anyone accused her of lying, and she had imagined herself to be a truthful person.

She wasn't. The guilt she felt spread over her like an inward stain, till she felt everyone must see her for what she was. The reason she did not normally tell lies was, she realised, because she had no reason to do so. And the first time real temptation had come her way, she had fallen into it so dreadfully easily.

The enjoyment had gone out of the evening for her. The flowers Marcus had given her already seemed to droop. The new Evie she had met for the first time today was the old Evie after all. The man she had hoped to surprise and enthrall despised her. The man she *had* attracted almost belonged to her best friend, and Sofia might never speak to her again.

If only she could go home now, and never see Rory McDermot again. If only she had worn her old dress, and Marcus hadn't noticed her.

If only Rory the Irishman wasn't so attractive, even when angry! His voice had music in it, and he seemed to be laughing somewhere inside himself, even when his face was grim and angry, his eyes as hard as stones.

She shivered in the warm evening, remembering the

43

other lie she had told. Not exactly a lie, for it was nothing but the truth. Her mother was expecting her father to arrive any day, but she had been expecting that for the past eleven years or so. Sooner or later that terrible man would find out.

Cautiously, she turned her head to look at him again. He had gone from the sea wall where she had left him. Gone where, and with whom?

'Oh, there you are!' said Marcus over her shoulder. 'Where did you get to? I wanted you to sit in my boat to watch the fireworks. Did you enjoy them?'

'They were fine, Marcus. Where's Sofia? Don't you think she looks pretty tonight?'

He grinned. His hair was black as carob-pods, and curled crisply, close to his head. His dark eyes travelled over her face, as if searching. 'Sofia's making eyes at the Irishman. He thinks she's pretty, judging by the way he was holding her when they danced just now. Didn't you see? Last night too.'

'He has good taste. He'd charm any girl, Marcus. You island men will have to watch out, or he'll whisk her away to his own country before you can stone an olive.'

Marcus sat up, and a small frown appeared between his strongly marked black brows. 'Will he? There are a few men here who'll see about that.'

So Marcus could be jealous, could he? Good. She added a little more fuel to the small fire by saying, 'He has a silver tongue, and she tells me he sings like an angel. Can you sing, Marcus?'

He scowled again. 'Certainly I can. Wait. Listen.' He strode off, and presently snatched a guitar from one of the players on the boat.

The fireworks being over, everyone was ready for more entertainment. Marcus sang well and was rewarded with applause and shouts. Someone thrust a glass of wine into his hand.

'Now the visitors,' Stratos shouted. 'Sing again, *kyrie*—the song you gave us last night.'

Eve clenched her hands tightly. Oh, no! Let Marcus have his triumph. This is his night.

But an expectant silence fell and into the scented darkness came a clear, trained tenor. A sad, homesick song floating over the water.

She is far from the land where her young hero sleeps.

What land? What young hero? Evie pressed her palms together, and tears trickled behind her eyes. The sadness in the voice chimed with her own unhappiness. He must, she thought, he must tell me the story of this song. I must know about the young hero and the lady who had to leave her own land. But how could she ask him? He had branded her as a liar, and liars he couldn't abide. And tomorrow or the next day, he would find out about her father. Everyone was happy here tonight. Her mother was chatting. Georgi and his friends were swimming in the warm dark water. Marcus was surrounded with friends, having apparently forgotten he had given his bouquet to Evie Marsden. And look at Sofia and Rory McDermot, laughing and sharing secrets as they danced the old-fashioned island dances!

She was the odd one out.

An older man asked her to dance, then one and another of the younger ones, and soon she was whirling as fast as anyone, more lightly than most, to the insistent beat of the local instruments. And then Marcus caught her again and danced with her until she was out of breath and obliged to sit down to recover.

'I hate you,' whispered Sofia close to her ear. 'I thought we were friends. I thought you knew I'd always wanted Marcus. If you don't want a man of your own, or can't get one, don't steal mine!'

Evie swung round, to face a Sofia she hardly recognised. The girl's face was distorted with hatred. 'I didn't steal him. He offered me the flowers. It's an insult to refuse a man's flowers, offered like that.'

'He can't look at anyone but you. You could discourage him if you were my true friend, like I thought you were.'

'Sofia,' Evie said firmly, 'if Marcus doesn't find you as attractive as you find him, that isn't my fault. Stop crying—you look terrible. And why cry anyway? You were getting on well enough with the Kyrios McDermot.'

'Only to make Marcus jealous. I wanted to hurt him.'

'Trying to make someone unhappy seems a funny way of loving him.'

'Don't you know, you can't show a man you love him? Not at first. You have to keep him guessing, and then choose the right moment for letting him know how you really feel. When you're certain you know how he really feels.'

'Wouldn't it be simpler to tell the truth, both of you? It would save a lot of worry and unhappiness.'

Sofia sighed. 'You're such a child, Evie. Don't you know anything? How will you ever get yourself a husband, if you go about it so stupidly?'

'I shall wait for a man who falls in love with me to come and ask me to marry him.'

'You'll be an old maid, then. Men don't want to get married. They have to be caught, like wild birds.'

Evie stood up. 'Catch yours, then, and tame him. I won't hinder. We're friends. Let's stay friends. Run home and tidy up your face, and I'll persuade my mother she's tired and wants to leave now. I'll get out of your way.'

'Well—' Sofia hesitated only a moment. 'It isn't as if you were dancing, is it? I mean, tonight isn't terribly important to you, like it is for me. You're sure you don't mind?'

Evie did mind. Very much. Only now, with the prospect of going home and leaving everybody enjoying themselves on the quay, did she understand how much she wanted to stay; and to ask the Irishman to explain his song to her.

Sofia, eager to go, still hesitated. 'You wouldn't lend me your red shoes, I suppose? I've never had red shoes.'

Without a word, Evie took off her shoes and handed them over.

'Thanks. Wait here and I'll bring you my sandals. You can't walk home in your best stockings.'

Sofia had no sooner disappeared than Rory McDermot stood before her.

'Will you dance with me, Princess?'

'I can't.'

'Because you are annoyed with me? Won't you take my olive branch? It's offered by way of apology. Only my aching bones spoke, I assure you.'

'You said nothing but the truth. I did lie to you. I meant to.'

He shrugged. 'Can't we both forget it? It's a heavenly night for dancing.'

'I'm sorry, I can't dance with you.'

He bowed stiffly. 'Very well. You prefer to swim alone. No doubt you prefer to dance alone, though it seems a pity when everyone else is dancing with a partner. Or is there another partner who likes to keep you to himself?'

She shook her head dumbly. It really was not

possible to explain how she came to be without shoes suddenly. Disappointment brought tears to her eyes. Why had she not understood earlier that what she wanted most in the world was to dance with the Irishman, wearing her scarlet shoes?

He stalked away stiff-legged and she knew in her bones, from the tilt of his head and the set of his shoulders, that he was hurt and angry with her stupid refusal to dance when everyone else was dancing.

I don't understand myself any more, she thought. Why couldn't I say simply that I had no shoes? We could have laughed about it, and waited for Sofia to come back with her sandals. What kept me silent, what made me hurt him like that? I really don't know what got into me.

When Sofia came tripping back, smiling and happy wearing the red shoes, Evie thrust her feet into borrowed sandals and went to saddle her mother's donkey. Even at the top of the path to the Villa Julia, the sound of music could still be heard, the lights still twinkled, reflected in the sea.

'Why did we have to come home so soon?' Georgi grumbled. 'I hadn't eaten nearly as many kebabs as I could have.'

Why indeed? Evie stared at the winking coloured lights below. What had gone wrong—and why?

Evie was milking the goats when she saw Rory McDermot come striding through the lemon trees. *He knows!* she thought with a sinking heart. She kept still and quiet, hoping he wouldn't see her in the dappled shadows of the wooden shelter, dazzled as he must be by the bright morning sun. But he came straight towards her, and leaned on the crooked doorpost looking in.

'No wonder you ran away, with another whopping

48

falsehood on your conscience! And living next door to the monastery, too, and those saintly old Brothers. What would they say if they knew?'

She kept on milking, not looking up. His shadow lay long and thin across the beaten earth floor.

'So your mother expects your father home any day?'

'It's the truth. She does.'

'Aye,' he said slowly, 'maybe it is. Maybe there was no need to add that she'd been doing just that for the past dozen years. When do *you* expect him?'

'Never. I think he's dead. He must be.'

He folded his long legs and sat beside her on a handful of clean straw. 'So?'

'I would like to be sure, for my brother's sake. It would make all the difference to him.'

'Why?'

'He'd be the head of the family, and my mother would respect his wishes.'

'Which are?'

'To keep his farm and his home. He has land of his own, which he wants to cultivate. He and I can do it together. We don't want to go elsewhere.'

'Isn't that rather limiting? A man should see the world.'

'You've seen the world. Why do you want to buy our house?'

'Primarily, to live in it.'

'There you are! You've seen the world and you'd live here if you could choose. So why can't you let Georgi alone? He's got what you want, and you are eager to push him out of it, for your own benefit.'

'A barbed point, my lady, and thrust deep. Can't you see it's different? I've made a choice. Georgi has had no choice. He gets his notions of England from you, I think?'

49

'I don't tell lies to him. He believes what I say. he's happy here, he has a future. Please go away and leave us in peace.'

He was silent a long minute. A goat bleated restlessly.

'What do you do with all this milk?'

'I make cheese. Oh, I'm sorry, I should invite you to breakfast—dates, our own cheese, and milk to drink. My mother makes good bread.'

'Thank you. I accept.'

'I wish you wouldn't. You mean to turn our lives upside down, don't you? I think I had a premonition, that first day when you landed on the quay. We don't want strangers on this island. We've had too many, in our history. Mostly they haven't been good for the islanders.'

'Strangers bring trade. Ask the men if they'll refuse that. If everybody thought as you do, you'd be living in caves up the mountain. You can't turn your back on civilisation, child. Don't be so narrow-minded.'

'Some people,' she said crossly, 'are so narrow-minded that they can't see anything but money, or hear anything but the rustle of money. Have you seen the tourist islands? Do they belong to the people any more? Leave us alone!'

His eyes having accustomed themselves to the deep shade, he could see her small passionate face, the tenseness of her slim body. He was moved with pity and regret. She could never win her single-handed fight against progress, and she was terribly wrong about her little brother. When would she understand that the handsome, sturdy boy would be a man sooner than she thought, and might then accuse her of having kept him ignorant and inexperienced, a farmer with a few acres, a few trees, a few goats? The mother was right about that.

Regret—that he was not five years younger, five years less experienced and world-weary. He saw himself as he had once been, riding his father's fine Connemara ponies along the Atlantic shore, young and free in the years before Clodagh; free as the gulls over the sea, and the piping oyster-catchers among the tangy wrack of the beach.

'You invited me to breakfast,' he reminded her gently.

Without a word, she put her milk-bucket by the wall and untied the goat. 'That's the last. I expect you find it a bit smelly in here. Most people do. We eat on the terrace. Come along.'

He took the bucket from her. 'Let me carry that.'

She followed him into the sun. 'You mean to buy our house, don't you?'

'I mean to try. It's what I had in mind and I can't let one girl with a lot of prejudices come between me and what I need. I've planned my future and somehow, somewhere, I shall carry my plans out. Besides—'

She took the bucket from him. 'In here. If you want to wash, there's water and soap on the table by the door. Besides what?'

'You're wrong about Georgi. Your mother is right. He must get away from here before he's too old to learn. And there's another thing you ought to know about me—'

'Evie? Is that you? Did you have trouble with the goats?' Julia came out into the yard. She had changed into her best black dress, put on an embroidered apron and a lace cap, Evie saw at once. So she had seen Rory come through the lemon trees and knew exactly what had detained her daughter.

In the harsh morning sun her face looked seamed and yellow. She's ageing, Evie thought with a stab of fear. But she can't be old? Not twenty years since she was a bride. Twenty years, so many of them lonely and hardworking. Poor Mama, she needs rest and security, not a peasant's life on the land. Am I cruel to her, my little Mama?

Julia advanced towards Rory, giving him a gracious welcome and inviting him to share the morning meal. Evie, she said, would make him an omelette. She brushed aside his protest.

'A man needs a good breakfast, my husband used to tell me. Evie will be happy to do it, and you and I will sit and talk while we wait. You are a traveller, like my husband. Who knows, you may have met him on your journeys.'

With gentle dignity, Julia led her guest away, and Evie heard their voices murmuring on the terrace; her mother's silvery tones, Rory McDermot's masculine voice striking a deeper chord. There was a lilt in his speech which fascinated Evie, a music she had heard in no English or American voice.

She whisked eggs angrily, aware that her mother had meant to get rid of her for a time, to have the visitor to herself. What were they talking about? It was unlikely that Julia would come at once to the question of selling the house. That wasn't the island way. There would be much delicate manoeuvring round the subject, long discussions into which others would be drawn—the priest, without question, and Julia's male kin. Even with a willing seller and a willing buyer, such an important transaction as buying a house might last a month. Once in a lifetime, perhaps, a man might have such important business, so it was not to be hurried. The utmost enjoyment must be squeezed out of every step of the slow progress.

Maybe, she thought as the golden eggs foamed in

the bowl, Rory would lose patience and go away. An Englishman certainly would. Name a price, say yes or no, and close the bargain—that was the English way.

She felt in her bones that the Irishman might be different. He gave the impression of living by God's time, as the islanders did. Time which could wait for a tree to blossom, fruit, and ripen its fruit; time which did not try to hurry the sun in the sky.

When she hurried on to the terrace with the perfectly-made omelette, the pair were sitting close together, Rory's head bent to listen to her mama.

He rose courteously, and pulled out a chair for her. 'Am I to eat this enormous omelette alone? You've brought only one plate.'

'We ate an hour ago. We are always up by sunrise, and try to finish the work before the sun gets hot. We are not so lazy as we appear to northern visitors, who lie in bed till seven or eight in the mornings. How long are you staying on the island, Mr. McDermot?'

Rory's eyebrows rose in surprise, finding her so dignified and distant suddenly. Milking the goat, she had seemed to him like a child. Now, straight-backed at the table, her golden hair smooth and a lace shawl thrown over her shoulders—which had not been there before, he felt sure—she was no child, but a gracious lovely lady. Suddenly it seemed important that he should know her age, but a man could hardly ask.

Julia answered for him. 'Mr. McDermot would like to stay a long time, if he could find a house for sale here. We were discussing the matter.'

'You have a house,' Evie said bluntly. 'The one by the harbour. That's just big enough for two people. He can buy that.'

'Two?' Rory asked.

'Well, I suppose you have a wife? Or perhaps you have a family and want something bigger?'

'I have no wife and no family.'

She cried, astonished, 'Then why do you want a house? You are free. You can live at the *taverna* as long as you wish, and leave any day you feel like leaving.'

'Evie,' her mother reproved, 'that is not our affair. It is not polite to question Mr. McDermot. It is enough to know that he wants a house. Why, is his concern.'

Embarrassed, Evie rose to pour fresh coffee. 'I'm sorry,' she murmured. 'It was just that I was surprised. You see, Mama, it is not a small house Mr. McDermot is looking for. He wants this house. *Our* house.'

Now it was his turn to look embarrassed. Evie smiled secretly to see his discomfiture, thinking it served him right for being so selfish. One man had no business trying to take away the home of a family.

One man? So he had no wife, and apparently no intention of bringing one to the island. The thought set her humming softly and to hide her quick surge of pleasure she ran to the edge of the terrace and pretended to look for Georgi. 'That boy! He's with the Brothers again, I'll be bound. They'll be busy, this hour in the morning, and he likes to help, Mr. McDermot. He'd be with them all day if he could.' She spoke challengingly, knowing he was against her in the matter of Georgi.

'Is that good for an eleven-year-old? A boy needs the company of younger men. Old Brothers in religion, worthy as they are, cannot teach him everything.'

Evie waved a hand in the direction of the village. 'Georgi is a friend of every man on the island, and every man is his father. They take him out in the fishing boats, and teach him about growing fruit, and

54

selling. This whole place is a school, for all the boys. We don't need a stranger to teach us how to bring up the children.'

Julia interrupted gently. She had been smiling from one to the other, as if unaware of the tension between her daughter and the visitor. 'All the same, child, your brother has an English father and he needs an English education. But that needs money and I have only enough to keep us here. When my husband comes home, of course he will pay. But, Kyrie McDermot, he is a little forgetful. A woman can wait twenty years, a man can wait five; but a child cannot wait at all. We must have the money *now*, to send the boy away. I have nothing to sell but the house and land.'

'You have a hard choice to make, Kyria. I am half a peasant myself, from the west of Ireland which is in some ways like your island. What will you live on, if you sell your land?'

'I have enough for myself, and a small place to live. Evie will get married, naturally. There is only Georgi's future to consider, and if my husband comes home and finds his son an ignorant islander, he will be angry with me. He set great store by the boy's education.'

'He should come back,' Evie muttered rebelliously. 'He has forgotten us. I don't mind it for myself, but he hurts my mother every day he stays away, and he is robbing his son.'

Rory tilted his chair on its back legs and stretched out his feet to the terrace edge. 'If you ask me, that boy should go to England or the States soon, befo.e he settles into the mould of a small farmer knowing nothing beyond the brim of his hat.'

Evie beat her fist on the table. 'No, no, *no*! Those boys would laugh at him and call him ignorant, because he wouldn't understand their stupid games. He swims like a fish, he speaks three languages

55

fluently, he knows a lot of history. Mr. McDermot, history was *born* here, all around the Mediterranean. Greece and Rome, the Ottoman empire, the Crusaders, the Venetians—we live with it. But Georgi has never played cricket or baseball, so he wouldn't be accepted by boys of his own age. Can't you understand how miserable he would be?'

Rory studied the angry girl gravely. 'Almost thou persuadest me. But just now I have business to talk over with your mother. Later, perhaps, you may be able to endure my company long enough to show me the monastery? Or don't they allow young females over their doorstep?'

He had the air of one humouring a child, buying its absence with the promise of a future treat. For a searing moment she was cruelly hurt and wanted to hurt him. It was years since she had thrown one of her wild tantrums, but now that old, almost uncontrollable rage rose up in her once more, and she had to fight for self-control, knowing that to lose her temper would be to lower herself still further in his eyes.

'The Brothers have a fine sense of hospitality, Mr. McDermot, and we are neighbours besides. My mama and I are always welcome under that roof, though at the moment I don't seem to be wanted under this.'

Head high, she marched angrily away. Only when she was safe in the wide dark kitchen did she let her fury have its way. She pressed her clenched fists to her temples, stamping her feet on the cool marble floor.

I hate him, I hate him! I won't endure being treated like a child. I'll never speak to him again. Never!

She ran out and through the lemon grove, making for the mountain above the house.

She climbed high and fast, till the exertion exhausted her anger, leaving her only with a strange, disturbed feeling she could not analyse. A feeling in which her fear of losing the Villa Julia had a part—and the memory of Marcus's dark eyes smiling into hers and the brief warm touch of their hands' encounter when he gave her the flowers. And the humiliation of being treated and spoken to like a child by the Irishman who seemed to be laughing at her all the time even when he spoke sharply, vexed by her childish lies.

In times of stress she had one refuge, the peak of the highest cliff on the island, where the land fell sheer into the sea as if a giant had sliced it off. A red cliff, which glowed at sunset like a jewel. There she would lie flat and inch forward to the very edge, and peep over the terrifying drop into the satin sea a dizzying distance below. The height made every nerve in her body crawl with fear, and her bare toes press hard into the barren rocks. Legend had it that long ago the islanders had punished wrongdoers by throwing them over to their death on the rocks below. Even now, though no one admitted it for fear of the kind old priest's disapproval, men and women would steal to the top and drop some valued possession into the sea with a prayer to the ancient gods for some much-desired favour; to the old gods whose time-fretted, headless statues still stood everywhere in the islands; so many still remaining after all these centuries, the Old Ones whose special care had been the silken Mediterranean, the dark wine, the olives, the jewelled islands blessed by the warm and lambent air. Was it possible, whispered some, that the Old Ones had forgotten their magic lands and their people?

Breathless at the top of her climb, she sat and hugged her knees, gazing down into the sea which was now quilted by a wisp of wind. When she heard footsteps on the bare pink rocks she turned quickly, half expecting Rory.

It was Marcus, mahogany-brown and deep-chested,

wearing only a pair of old faded shorts and canvas shoes.

'Evie! What are you doing there! Come back. Girls shouldn't sit so near the edge. You might get dizzy and fall over.'

'I always sit here. I'm not in the least dizzy. When we were younger you threatened to push me over, do you remember?'

He grinned cheerfully. 'I remember. You'd bitten me. You had sharp little teeth.' He eased himself to the ground beside her, avoiding a grey thistle with long thorns as fine as needles. 'You're a mystery, Evie. How is it Sofia is a woman grown, ready for marriage and children, and you—' his eyes travelled over her appraisingly. 'You are a child still. At least, you are today. The other night, in your blue dress and red shoes, I thought you were grown-up too. Then suddenly you changed back into the old Evie and ran away.'

'Like Cinderella.'

He looked blank. 'Who's she?'

'A girl in a story. She changed back into her ordinary self and ran away from a prince—a young man who thought she was grown-up.'

'What did he do?' An islander loved a story. Marcus bit a long thorn with his broad white teeth and looked at her expectantly.

'Went to look for her. But he didn't find her till the grown-up shoe she'd kicked off fitted her. He didn't want anybody else, so he had to wait and search.'

The young man nodded. 'No one else would do. What if another man found her first?'

'He probably worried about that, too, but it isn't mentioned in the story. Where is Sofia today?'

He scowled. 'Working at home. Her father beat her black and blue last night.'

'Poor Sofia!'

'She deserved it. She's been making a fool of herself with that Kyrios McDermot, going everywhere with him and not attending to her duties. They went off on a picnic together yesterday, took the boat and went swimming, when her mother needed her for whitewashing the house.'

'With Kyrios McDermot? So why beat poor Sofia? Why not beat him?'

'A man does what he wants to do. McDermot is on holiday and a guest at the *taverna*. It was Sofia's duty to tell him she was needed for whitewashing.' He was sulking, looking so like Georgi when deprived of a treat that Evie felt elder-sisterly and teased him.

Staring out to sea, she said lightly, 'Such an outing would be worth a beating or two.'

'You'd go with him?'

'I wasn't invited.'

He pressed the point. 'But if he did invite you?'

'I'd tell him I had work to do.'

'You wouldn't. You'd do as Sofia did. What's so wonderful about a stranger? Island girls should go with island boys.'

Evie felt sick with jealousy. It was a sensation new to her and she found it disagreeable. Rory was hers. He had held her in his arms for a fleeting moment, though by accident. He had called her a goddess and a princess. In spite of his tiresome urge to buy the Villa Julia, he was the first man who had ever interested her as a man and it was for him she had gone down to the waterfront in the blue dress and red slippers. So why couldn't Sofia content herself with Marcus and keep her little brown paws off Rory? Island girls should go with island boys.

'I agree entirely. So why don't you cut him out, Marcus? You're better-looking and probably richer, and Sofia likes you very much. You upset her by giving me the flowers. Why didn't you give them to her?'

'I meant to,' he admitted, grinning. 'Then—there you were! You took my breath away.'

She stared at an eagle wheeling like a speck in the wide blue expanse of sky. 'Would you marry me, Marcus?'

'Have you a dowry?'

'Certainly I have. Did you think I wouldn't have? Well? Would you marry me?'

He tilted his handsome head back and looked up at her under lowered lids. 'You're not strong enough.'

She stretched out her hands and stared at them. 'What do you mean? I work as hard as anybody else.'

'I plan to have my own restaurant soon. That's killing work for both husband and wife. I want a lot of children, too, sons to keep me in my old age. No, I'm sorry, you won't do, Evie.'

She laughed. 'Sofia could do it. And she's prettier than I am.'

He said glumly, 'I know. She's one of us—hard as nails for working, and more—' he shrugged, 'more to hug. She'd be a more comfortable wife. You'll always be skinny, Evie.'

'I'm not skinny, I'm slender—that's different. You really want Sofia, don't you? Well then, go and get her.'

The boy hesitated. 'I'm not sure. You're so beautiful, Evie. I could work twice as hard. I could—'

She sprang up. Far below, the monastery lay like a white cube of sugar glistening in the sun. Four toy figures crossed the courtyard, their shadows like black pins. Three were monks, the other was Rory McDermot.

'No, Marcus, I won't work myself into the ground helping you to run a restaurant. One day soon you'll be fat and lazy, and Sofia will do all the work for you and give you lovely children with eyes like yours. It's not for me. When I marry, I'll need to find another kind of husband altogether.'

He eyed her frankly. 'Not in that dress, Evie. You're a wild thing, aren't you? A dreaming girl with her ears full of the sea and her eyes full of the sky. Why don't you grow up?'

She watched the four black shadows cross the white yard. Nothing had been the same with her since the Irishman came to the island. Even if he now went back to his own country without even saying goodbye to her, she would never be quite the same again. He had called her a princess and stirred her out of her dream.

It was a long time before she answered Marcus, and by then he was striding off down the hill, leaping from stone to stone in his hurry.

'Grown up? I rather think I have, Marcus. And I don't think I'm going to like it at all.'

But the words fell between the soaring eagle and the sea.

Realising she was alone, Evie laughed. Marcus would comfort poor bruised Sofia before nightfall unless he sprained an ankle in his hurry to get down to her.

Then she lay flat and crept to the rim of the great red cliff.

Peering over, she let the terror of the height and the crawling water below take possession of her. This must be how eagles saw the land and sea below them.

What was Rory saying to the monks?

Had her mother agreed to sell the house? If so—if so—

She had promised Georgi to do anything in her power to save his house, but she had no power. None at all. The Villa Julia was not hers and if her mother chose to sell she could not prevent it happening.

She still wore the tiny Maltese cross round her neck, true to her resolve to wear it always now. Reluctantly she took it off and held it out over the water.

'Goddess of wisdom, please tell me what to do, and I'll do it. I promise you I will. Just give me an idea, or bring my father back in time if you can.' She had an idea that the bit about her father ought to be addressed to another god, but she had only one sacrifice.

With a tiny flash of light, the necklace disappeared. She lost sight of it long before it reached the sea.

CHAPTER FOUR

RORY and Brother Barnabas paced the shaded cloister. Barnabas was younger than Rory expected, aged in appearance by a long beard and black robe, tall black headdress and fluttering veil. To have such a man, of great wisdom and cultured mind, as neighbour increased Rory's longing to own the Villa Julia.

'You and the mother are right.' The monk's English was fair, though now and again he used Greek. 'The boy should see something of the world. Evie too. Exos is not one of the famous islands. We do not attract tourists, but it has its own charm. For your purpose, it is perfect.' He paused, to examine a pomegranate tree carefully. 'We have nothing on Exos to draw pilgrims, but we pray that one day St. Polystemon will come home—a local boy, martyred here on his own island a thousand years ago. If we had his skull, which now rests in a Cyprus monastery, he might work miracles for us. Then the pilgrims would flock, and with them would come more prosperity. Not that we, the Brothers, want prosperity. We are vowed to poverty. But the people are poor, and our young men have to leave us to get work and good wages.'

'I'm a God-fearing man, but I don't believe miracles happen anywhere, these days.'

'They don't, for the people who don't believe in them. The miracle-working relics never work for tourists. They think the power lies in the belt, the skull, the hole in the pillar. It lies in the mind, sir.'

'In the minds of ignorant peasants?'

Brother Barnabas smiled remotely. 'Never underrate

the poor and ignorant, *kyrie*. You may teach them much about book-learning, no doubt. But they could teach you much about faith. The relic of a saint merely serves as an aid to concentration. Any small object would do. So the skull of our St. Poly would work miracles here, because we all love him and trust him.'

'Wouldn't the other monastery give him to you?'

'Alas, even monks need money, if only to keep the roof on. We should have to pay them for St. Poly. Where is such a poor island as this to raise the price?'

Rory brought the conversation firmly back to the subject nearest his thoughts. 'Evie is determined the house should not be sold. I am equally determined to buy it. But if the mother spends the proceeds on the boy, what will they live on? That bothers me.'

'It's no problem. The son will support his mother. The girl will marry. She has a dowry.'

But marry whom? Rory paced beside the monk, turning that over in his mind. The life of a married woman in this part of the world could be hard. Too much work, in the house and field. Too many babies. Often a lazy husband, to be waited on hand and foot. In early middle age, many became worn-out drudges. Evie deserved better. But if few strangers came to Exos, or if she didn't get away soon, there might be no other choice for her. The thought hit him like a blow over the heart.

'Will the father ever return?' he wondered aloud.

Barnabas considered the question in his slow way. 'We talked much, the Kyrios Marsden and I. He had some property in England, but I always felt he went only to settle his affairs and come back. That he failed to do so suggests to me that he is dead.'

'Why have no enquiries been made, all these years?'

'Julia is a daughter of the Middle East. She accepts her husband's decrees without question. The ways of a man and his wife are unknown to me, but I do remember my mother never asked my father whether he would be gone a day, a week, or an hour. Nor did he ever think of telling her.'

'Evie is asking.'

'She is half English. She won't be content to wait now she is eighteen. She will make it her business to find out.'

Rory stared at the monk. 'Eighteen? But surely she can be no more than sixteen? She's a woman masquerading as a child, and I thought her a child masquerading as a woman! They will do it, Brother. One day one thing. Another day, quite another. At least a man knows where he is with a good horse or a good dog. Most of the beauty and none of the mystery. That girl reminds me of my young sister in many ways.'

He meant, she reminds me of Clodagh, in our golden days, when she was sixteen and I just turned twenty. All that long summer spent together, sailing, fishing, swimming. The smell of horses, the smell of the seaweed tangle, the smell of Clodagh's hair blowing across my face.

Brother Barnabas smoothed his beard with a thin hand. 'You seem disturbed?'

'I've been talking to her as if she were my kid sister. Only this morning I sent her packing because I had business to discuss with her mother. I half saw it, and still let myself be fooled. I should have known better. I remember—'

What did it matter to a monk, that he remembered the first day Clodagh seemed to him grown-up? Almost overnight, she had done something mysterious to herself . . . or perhaps it was the soft look in her eyes and about her mouth that changed her. That was the day he first understood he loved her as a man loves the woman he will marry. He discovered later it was the first day she met the Englishman who was now her husband.

The monk chuckled. 'Julia is a kindly hen with a pair of cygnets. The children have the mind and blood of their father in them. He was a fine man—big, handsome, generous of nature. I do what I can for his son, but it is not enough. If there is anything you can do—'

'I offered to rent the house. But to carry out Julia's plans, she needs a substantial lump sum. Education in England is expensive if you pay for it. Or it is free. Either he would have to go to a boarding school, or one of them would have to make a home for him over there. There's the matter of examinations, too, she seems not to understand. The English are great on their examinations. The whole project is more difficult than she imagines. There are fares. And clothes.'

Barnabas stopped his pacing. 'Georgi is intelligent and has been well grounded. If his father is dead, he is also a landowner. He needs nothing England can give him, except a wider experience of life. If that is to be, God will attend to it. Now it is time I went to my prayers. Our hours are not our own, but God's. If you care to join us in our chapel, you're welcome.'

'Thank you. Will you answer one more question? Kyria Julia has invited me to move in to the villa. The *taverna* is noisy, and I can't work there. The offer of a big quiet room over the sea is tempting. Would the island sanction such a move?'

'Wise man! You feel your way carefully, eh? Yes, you could do that without causing gossip. Julia is above reproach, well respected. She is, you understand, related to almost every family on Exos.'

Rory nodded. He knew about small communities and had guessed as much.

'And as to buying the house? It is what I dreamed of, and if I scoured the whole Mediterranean I could not find anything nearer my mind. But I don't want to rush the family into doing something they will later regret.'

'There will be no rush, *kyrie*. There will be a go-between appointed, and the talking will go on for weeks. Julia will have advice from every man and woman in the place, and in the end will make up her own mind. Make her an offer for it if you really want it, and leave the outcome in the hands of God.'

Between noon and three, at this time of year, the island slept. A soft mist blurred the sharp shadows; the tiny wavelets died to nothing and the boats lay motionless over their reflections in still water. The birds slept, the trees slept and it seemed as if even the air slept. On the whole of Exos, no one moved except under dire compulsion.

Evie left the top of the huge cliff and sought out her private retreat, a small deserted temple heavily over-grown, where four headless statues of Greek gods had stood for more than two thousand years. This had been her playroom as a child, the four vast draped figures her friends and companions. She had never minded that they had no heads, for her imagination provided them with friendly faces and voices to match their sturdy bodies and firmly-planted bare feet. They had always been more real and everyday than the bodiless saints, big-eyed and hungry-looking, that she saw on the icons in the church and monastery. Here she curled up and went to sleep in the shade. The still air was heavy with the scent of wild flowers.

She woke suddenly, realising she had slept longer than usual and her mother might be wondering where she was, and would be wanting her afternoon coffee. The peace of the empty temple had soothed away the burning anger, and she was prepared to accept some blame herself. She rested her chin on her knees, and conducted a conversation with the four gods as she had done as a child.

'Your fault,' said the armless woman who had such splendid stone feet. 'Go to Kyrenia tomorrow and buy yourself some proper clothes. It's time you behaved like a young lady. Look at *me*.'

'Your fault,' said the deep-chested man whose left leg was cut off below the knee. 'You should do something about your father. Find out if he's still alive, and tell him to come home.'

'But where, and how, shall I find him?' She must have spoken aloud, for an echo came back. It brought no answer.

Yet when she reached the house, the answer was in her head. It was so simple. Tomorrow she would take the daily caique to Kyrenia, buy some dress material for herself, and a pattern; and then consult a lawyer. If he didn't know how to trace a lost father, he would at least know how to contact someone who would tell her.

Her hand on the latch of the door, she threw a glance over her shoulder at the summit of the mountain, where a knowledgeable eye could just detect the ruin. 'Thank you,' she said in a whisper. 'I'll take your advice.'

Her mother was talking, in her visitor-English. When Evie entered the big blue-painted room she saw Rory McDermot. He stood up when she entered. The small courtesy made her vividly conscious of her dusty bare feet.

They were drinking coffee, eating the tiny almond and honey cakes her mother made for special occasions.

'The *kyrios* has accepted my invitation to stay here, Evie,' Julia said, half nervously. 'He is a writer, did you know? The *taverna* is noisy and there is no table in his room. We have your father's room vacant, so why should he not move in? There is a desk by the window, and a view over the sea. Of course, he understands that he must move out at once, if your father comes home.'

'Of course,' Rory murmured. 'And if you would call me Rory I should feel myself at home. You don't mind, Miss Marsden?'

Evie's eyes widened. In her whole life, no one had ever addressed her as Miss. 'You are welcome,' she murmured formally. 'May your stay be a happy one.'

'Thank you.'

The conversation flagged. Julia put in a few stitches at the embroidery in her frame.

'You visited the Brothers?' Evie said at last, in her best English.

Rory nodded. 'And had a long talk with Barnabas.'

'About us?'

'About everything under the sun, which includes you, naturally. He is fond of young Georgi, and thinks him a clever boy. We also spoke of the lemon trade and he gave me a good recipe for dumplings for soup.'

Evie searched her mind for new topics of conversation. She had never suffered from shyness, having had nobody of whom she need be shy. So she did not recognise the condition immediately, and blamed herself for lack of hospitality.

'I'll show you my private temple if you like.' As soon as the words were out, she regretted them. Her temple was her own.

'I'd like that very much. Unless it is near the coppermines.'

She looked up sharply and caught a smile in his eyes. Then suddenly he laughed and she laughed with him, till Julia stared at the pair of them in bewilderment.

'What is funny about the coppermines?' she asked plaintively.

A clatter from outside answered her. 'That's Georgi. Why can't that boy arrive without making such a noise? I sent him down to the village with a note to the priest and my cousin Stephanos, and told him to wait for an answer.'

Evie drew a long breath. Her mother's cousin was famous for his skill as a go-between. So was the priest, for holding the scales fairly between buyer and seller. Two such formidable persons approached by Julia at one and the same time could only mean one thing. Quick anger mounted in the girl. Had her mother decided to sell the house, Georgi's land, without consulting her? Without making any real attempt to find George Marsden, whose home, after all, the Villa Julia was?

'What answer?' she said in a low tense voice. 'What do you want of Cousin Stephanos?'

Julia was tart. 'That's my business.'

'Is it, Mama? Are you sure? Isn't it perhaps Rory's business also? What were you and he talking about, this morning?'

She knew her mother's mood, a curious mixture of outward meekness and inward stubbornness which meant she intended to do, or already had done, something of which her family would probably not approve.

Before Julia answered, Georgi came in with a note. 'This is from the priest, and Uncle Stephanos didn't write, but he says he'll do it if you are sure you know your own mind, and if the foreigner can pay a good price.'

'I can pay a fair price,' Rory put in quietly, and Julia crimsoned.

'So I'm right?' Evie looked from one to the other, 'You mean to buy our house and turn us out, Mr. McDermot? You've crept in here and talked my mother into selling, having first got rid of me because you knew neither my brother or I want to lose our home and land. Now I find you've even got yourself into the house as a lodger. Couldn't you wait till the whole place was yours? Do you have to come lording it before the sale has been properly discussed?'

'I *have* discussed it,' Rory told her sharply, the laughter gone from his eyes. 'With the owner. I offered your mother a price this morning, but she quite properly prefers me to discuss terms with her representatives. She won't be talked into selling, nor would I dream of doing so unless she is advised by her family. The grown-up members of it,' he added pointedly.

'What do my uncles care? It's Georgi I'm worried about. Because he's only a child, must he lose his land? Mama, I demand that Georgi has a representative too. Someone to speak for him in his interests.'

Julia's mouth was set stubborn. 'It's my house, my land. I make the decisions, in your father's absence. And I say my husband's wishes must be carried out; he always talked of an English education for his son.'

'I won't go,' Georgi said, as stubborn as his mother—looking, Evie noticed suddenly, very like her, with the same thrust-out jaw and set of the head. 'You can't make me learn anything, even if you can force me to go to an English school. Your money will be wasted, every *mil* of it.'

'Don't dare to speak to me—your *mother*—like that! You're a baby yet. You'll do exactly as I say, or I shall beat you.'

'Beat me, then! I don't care, I don't care!' The boy was sobbing hysterically. He swung round suddenly and flew at Rory, pounding the man with his clenched fists. 'Go away! It's your fault. Why did you come here? Get away from us, do you hear? We don't want you!'

Rory caught the flailing wrists, held the boy away

from him till he ceased struggling and stood still, crimson-faced and gasping.

'That's better,' Rory said quietly. 'Now I suggest you apologise to your mother for that outbreak. Then you and I will go outside and have a talk about it, man to man. We might stroll up to the monastery and discuss it with your friends there, eh?'

'No. I won't speak to you again, ever. And I won't have you living in my house!'

'Mama's house,' Evie reminded him. 'Losing your temper won't help, darling. If it would, I'd lose mine. Come with me. Let's go up the mountain and think. But first apologise to Mama.'

Rory massaged his chin thoughtfully. 'Who started it, mavourneen? You are a bit of a rebel yourself. You set the example.'

Evie put an arm round Georgi's shoulder and met Rory's gaze firmly. 'Very well. We both apologise for being rude to Mama. But not to you. Georgi is right, all this trouble is your fault. I'd be obliged if you would go away and leave us in peace, as we were before you came. We don't want you.'

Rory reached for a dilapidated straw hat which he clapped on his head at an angle. 'Very well, ma'am, I'll go. Kyria Julia, my offer is withdrawn. I am defeated by your children. I can't bring myself to take the roof from over their heads. I'll leave the island by tomorrow's boat.'

He bowed to Julia, and ignoring the brother and sister, marched out of the house and into the white sun. His brisk feet set up little spurts of dry red soil as he went. He whistled a lilting tune.

'Look what you've done, you ungrateful children!' Julia began to cry.

'Good riddance,' said Evie hardly.

She watched her enemy out of sight. There was

something about the hunch of a shoulder, the tilt of a head, the sound of that gay little whistle, that gripped her heart. A man defeated, and not showing it. Hurt, and trying not to care. A man whose dream had fallen about his ears, and he making the best of things.

Almost, she opened her mouth to call him back. Then, catching sight of Georgi's distressed face, the soft mouth quivering but pressed shut, she hugged the boy again and dropped a light kiss on his tousled hair.

'Maybe we were hard on him, little brother. The war isn't won yet. I fancy he'll be back some day.'

She knelt by her mother's chair and took the work-worn hands in her own. 'Mama, I'm sorry. Did it mean so much to you? If only my father were here! How could he—how could he leave us like this? Dear Mama, don't you see, we can't go on for ever, waiting for him to come back. We must make some effort to find out what happened to him. Let me try.'

Julia covered her face and sobbed silently, with quiet despair. Evie motioned to the boy to go away. Then she waited patiently till grief had exhausted itself.

'What is it, Mama? Do you know something you haven't told us? I've never seen you cry like this before. You are always so hopeful and so confident. You will let me try to find him?'

'But that would be to admit I doubted him. My belief in George is all I have. Don't you understand that? To admit doubt—what would that do to my pride? Everybody would be saying *Julia's afraid he's left her!* And from that, it's only a step to everybody saying *He has left her.* I couldn't bear that. He was such a good man, and so happy to be here with us. He really loved us.'

'In that case, I think he must be dead. I'm sorry, Mama, but we must face it and not pretend any more. Let me go to a lawyer in Kyrenia and ask him to make inquiries in England. There must be ways of finding out, which we don't know.'

'You'd take my hope away from me.'

'I know, love. But isn't it better to know the truth?'

'Young people are for knowing the truth, however cruel. All right, go and ask, if the truth is what you want. You're not old enough to be glad of a veil over the face of reality; when you've faced the truth often enough and long enough, you won't be so eager to see it naked. Go with my blessing. You'll need some money, won't you?'

'Yes, please. And also—' Evie pulled at her shabby skirt—'I need something to wear, Mama. I'll make myself some dresses if you'll help me. We could get out the old sewing machine, couldn't we?'

'Yes, of course. I've neglected my daughter. We must think about a husband for you, and that means pretty dresses. One of the Brothers will oil the machine and get it working again. Your father bought it for a wedding present, you know.'

Julia cheered up with the thought of dresses to make, and began to talk of likely young men on the island. 'But you're not the sort to marry an island man, Evie. Too much like your father. We must have something better for you. Perhaps we should wait till George comes home?'

Her eyes filled with tears again as she remembered that old excuse for postponing action would no longer be acceptable to her children.

'Well, all the same, I think you should meet more nice families. If only you'd let me sell the house, you could use the money to take Georgi to England, and maybe get work there for a while. You're a good cook, and awfully clever with the goats and with growing things. Or you could teach Greek, couldn't you? In a school? George used to say English schools always taught Latin and Greek, though what they wanted to speak Latin for, I can't imagine.'

'Not modern Greek, I believe, Mama. The old Greek that nobody knows any more.'

'Really? How stupid! Two languages nobody wants to know? Perhaps English schools are not so good after all.'

'Perhaps they have different ideas now.'

'Or you could go to Athens and teach English. Your father was very particular about your having a good accent.'

Evie left her mother preparing *moussaka* for the evening meal, attended to the goats, then walked slowly down to the sea. A broad stripe of gold lay across the blue, the last of the day's sun—a path, she used to think, to adventure somewhere beyond the horizon.

And now, when she was old enough to take the path, and her mother willing to let her go, she no longer wanted it. Life felt flat, dull, and lacking in all excitement. Why can't I be like Sofia, she thought crossly, and excited at the thought of going to Kyrenia tomorrow to buy material for new dresses? It isn't as if I wanted to stay here any more. Even my beloved Exos suddenly seems empty. I feel hollow; as if my heart had gone out of my body.

She kicked off her sandals and walked along the beach, letting the tiny edge of foam roll up over her ankles. She wondered about her father. What had taken him away so suddenly? Why had he not come back? What could there be, anywhere in the whole world, more beautiful than Exos, the Villa Julia, his wife and children? Where could life be easier, with the sun to ripen his lemons; the little stream which never dried up, to water his vegetables; the vine shading the terrace, where in autumn the ripe grapes hung down so one did not even have to stretch to reach them?

What could have drawn a man away from all this?

The rim of the sun touched the sea. It would be quite dark soon. She turned back, trailing her feet in the water. All this thought about her father had been a barrier, put up to keep Rory McDermot out of her mind.

Now she let him in. If the young are the only ones brave enough to face naked truth, let me face it.

I love Rory McDermot. It is because he is going that the island lacks excitement. Because he won't be there, that Athens seems just a dreary bore. Because he won't see them, that new dresses are not worth bothering with.

I love him.

She said the words out loud, as softly as the plash of golden sea round her ankles. I sent him away, with unkind words in his ears. He could have lived in the house, I could have seen him every day; made his bed, done his washing, served his food. He might have loved me. We might have been married and lived in the house, and he could have had his dream after all, and—

The sun went down. Where all had been light, now there was not even twilight, but only a grey land and a grey sea, which in a minute would be quite dark.

What a fool—what an utter fool I have been!

Forgetting her sandals, she raced home. Georgi was lighting lanterns on the terrace, and the good, familiar smell of *moussaka* came from the kitchen.

Rory scrambled down the steep path which led to the village. He was somewhat downcast by the quick turn of events at the Villa, but he felt in his bones that all was not lost. So he whistled a cheerful jig as he went. He'd be back. The mother was for him. The boy was influenced by his sister, and she was a lass of determination and character. A good hot temper besides, he reflected. Plenty of spirit.

Well, well, we shall see, he thought. He'd had plenty

of experience taming fine young horses full of spirit and fight, and he learnt patience the hard way. There came a moment to leave the young creature alone, to walk away, to wait. And nine times out of ten, if a man had the patience, its own curiosity about the strange power which it had felt for the first time would bring it back. He saw them now, the shining red horses on the green grass, bright in the soft Irish sunlight; delicately stepping, fine nostrils flaring, curiosity and the hidden desire to be mastered bringing them pace by pace towards the man they feared yet longed for.

He had almost reached level ground when Marcus stepped from behind a stand of elephant grass, and stood in the way, glowering.

'*Kalispera*,' said Rory, deceptively gentle. A sixth sense warned him that the young man meant trouble. Something in the way he hunched those powerful shoulders, or a leery look in the eyes, perhaps. The Irishman stood his ground, muscles tensed for action. He hated trouble, and would go out of his way to avoid it. Yet not too far out. Not far enough to discommode himself.

'Time you left Exos, Irishman,' Marcus said bluntly. 'I suggest you take tomorrow's boat if you want to keep out of trouble.'

Rory nodded agreeably. 'That's the second invitation I've had today to leave the island. I really think I might. Only—' he smiled apologetically, 'it's one of the defects in the Irish character that when asked politely to do a thing, we want to know why. Why do *you* want me to leave? You might as well tell me. I'm a reasonable man—within reason.'

'Sofia is my girl and always has been. Keep off her, that's all. She's so taken up with you, she can't see sense. I mean to marry her, understand? So the sooner you're out of sight the sooner she'll listen to me and we can get back to Greece and start looking for a restaurant to buy.'

'Does she know that?'

'She won't listen. Too busy washing your shirt, or cooking your meal, or cleaning your room, or waiting on you at table. If she's not dancing with you or taking you out in her father's boat.'

Rory stroked his chin thoughtfully. 'So? The girl is overdoing it, eh? And you haven't told her you want to take her off to Greece?'

'No, I haven't. What do you mean, overdoing it?'

Rory tapped the angry man on the chest. 'I mean, my dear sir, that the girl is head over heels in love with you. That she wants nothing else in life but to leave the island and see the world. And that she's been using me, with my connivance, I admit, to make you jealous. With a view to making you fall in love with her. It seems she's been successful.'

Marcus's jaw dropped. 'The little—! The deceiving little monkey! I came home for the special purpose of marrying her, if she'd grown into a woman capable of helping me with the restaurant and giving me good sons. A man can't marry a weakling, you know. If she'd only given me a chance—!'

'Your fault,' Rory reminded him. He could breathe easier now. There would be no need to fight Marcus. He could have licked the boy, he thought—just. He had the advantage of being lighter on his feet, more experienced, and maybe a shade tougher. But he disliked fighting, being bone lazy. 'You gave Evie those flowers, which properly upset the applecart.'

Marcus frowned. 'Apples? There were no apples. That was Evie's fault for looking so—different. She's beautiful, that girl.'

'So I've noticed.'

'She has a dowry too. She told me. But not strong

enough for me, *kyrie*. It's plump little Sofia I want. That girl is as strong as a horse, and—' he grinned suddenly, 'I like them plump.'

The two men walked towards the village. 'What you must do now,' Rory counselled, 'is to show your hand. Stand no nonsense from the girl. She will come running if you so much as crook your little finger.'

'I'll do it. And you'll leave the island?'

Rory halted. 'We—ell, there's a difficulty, Marcus. It's another defect in the Irish character, I'm afraid. When asked to do a thing twice, we think there must be some good reason for *not* doing it. So we don't. It makes life difficult for us, but there it is. I'm sorry about that, but I simply can't go now.'

'We could make you—the Exos men. Without a word said or a blow struck, we could make you leave tomorrow.'

'You could, boy, you could. But it would do you no good with the lady, and you know it. Look, I have a better plan. I think I owe you something. So far, I've played the game on Sofia's side. Now it's time to play on yours. It's rather f-funny, don't you think—'

Suddenly Rory began to laugh, seeing the absurdity of the situation. He bent double with laughter, and tears filled his eyes. Marcus watched amazed, but the laughter proved infectious. Slowly, he chuckled. In a moment both men were helpless. Rory punched Marcus feebly, struggling to control his voice.

'You've got to come out on t-top, see? The big hero. So tonight—' he paused to mop his eyes with a grubby handkerchief, 'I'll eat outside. If Sofia is on duty—'

'She will be, if you're there. Don't fear for that!'

'I'll make a fuss of her. Invite her to join me for a bottle of wine. She'll play along if you're watching.'

Marcus looked doubtful. 'Are you sure it will work? What do I do?'

'You march up and tell me to clear off. Throw out your chest, flex your muscles and look dangerous. You can do it?'

'Sure I can. And you?'

'I go. I don't argue, but pay my bill and leave. Then you sit down in my place—and bob's your uncle.'

'My uncle? What has he to do with it?'

'I mean, you're all right. The girl wants no one but you, Marcus. She's a charmer, I admit. As attractive and merry a little creature as a man could wish to meet, and I can't think why I've never so much as kissed her. But she's yours, man, if you can talk your way out of that business of giving the flowers to the wrong girl. All right?'

Marcus obviously liked the idea. A slow grin spread over his face. 'She's been playing a trick on me, eh? Now you and I—' he thumped Rory's arm with a hard clenched fist, 'will pay her back in her own coin, eh? A trick. Yes, that's good, *kyrie*.' He laughed again. 'Now we'll separate. It would not do, to walk into the village together like old friends.'

After supper, Georgi drew Evie on one side and whispered, 'Where did he go? He said he wanted to talk to *me*, man to man. You had no right to send him away.'

'You yourself told him to go.'

'That was before. Men should talk over these things. I would have gone with him, but you interrupted and said I had to go with you, up the mountain. There's too much women's talk going on. Tomorrow I'm going down to see the Kyrios McDermot, whatever you say.'

'You mean you've changed your mind about England?'

'No, I won't go. But I'm not big enough yet to run everything myself, and you and Mama are only women. I bet that man has some good ideas, if everybody stopped shouting and listened to him. There's no harm in talking to him, is there?'

'N-no, I suppose not. But listen, Georgi. We need our father now, and I'm going to find him. Tomorrow I'm going to Kyrenia and I'll find a lawyer to act for us. And down there on the beach I had another idea. I think I know how to fix everything.'

'What idea? Will it work?'

Evie crushed her doubts. It had to work. 'Don't be too hopeful. But it might. Someone—some woman—has to run this house for him if he buys it. He's not married. He hasn't any sweetheart, at least I don't think he has, and I'm sure I should have known by the way he spoke.'

'How soon will you know whether it works or not?'

The girl swallowed nervously. 'Tonight. It must be tonight, because I think he'll leave Exos tomorrow.'

'Why worry, then? If he's leaving, we needn't bother.'

Evie drew him closer to her. How slight he was still, the bone and muscle of a man not yet developed. Yet already he thought like a man, not a child. He had begun to shake off the rule of women, like a true islander. Mama's reign was over, though she didn't suspect it yet.

'Little king,' Evie whispered, 'we're not out of danger. Mama has her heart in this business and if it isn't Rory McDermot it might be someone much worse. So let me try my plan tonight.'

'All right. And if it doesn't work, I'll talk to him tomorrow before the boat leaves.'

She shook her head violently. 'No, no. No. This is all or nothing. One throw of the dice. If we lose, we lose.

If he doesn't agree to my suggestion, he'll never come back, and you must never ask him. Promise.'

'Tell me what it is, your plan?'

'No, that I can never tell anyone. Only him.' She laid her finger on the boy's lips. 'Not a word to Mama, Georgi. I'll say I'm going down to talk to Sofia about the dress materials.'

At the edge of the village, the enormity of what she had come to do brought Evie to a halt. She leaned against a date-palm in the darkness, listening to the voices, the chink of bottles and glasses. Her hands were damp, her mouth dry with nerves. Her heart beat fast and she found it hard to breathe.

She must go back to Georgi and tell him she had failed, had not even had the courage to put her idea into practice. Why hadn't she realised, back there on the beach, that it was impossible? It had seemed such a simple business transaction when she first thought of it. Now—she swallowed, her throat stiff.

Peering round the thick trunk of the tree, she saw Rory at a table which bore the remains of an evening meal. She watched him, seeing no one else though most of the tables were occupied. Then Sofia came, wearing her best Sunday dress for work and skimming through the crowd to Rory's table.

The expression on her friend's face spoke volumes. She wants *Rory*, Evie whispered to herself. Not Marcus. That's how she used to look when she talked about Marcus, but now it's Rory. That's why she risked the beating. She really has changed. Poor Marcus!

Poor Sofia! For Rory would never choose her. I know that much about him now.

Sofia set down a fresh bottle and a second glass on Rory's table. Then, half rising, the man put his arm round her waist and drew her down. Heads close, they laughed together, and Rory's hand went to the bottle to fill both glasses.

Faces close together across the table, the pair touched glasses and drank, in a gesture as intimate as a kiss.

Evie turned away with a choking sob. She ran till she was out of breath, then flung herself down on the stony path and pressed her face into her hands.

To have sent Rory away so unkindly was bad enough. But then she had had the secret hope—almost the certainty—that he would come back. At the time she had not known it consciously, but now the knowledge stabbed her cruelly. She had been so sure, so ridiculously sure.

But to know that the man she loved was sitting there laughing with Sofia, the pair of them making pictures in each other's eyes over a glass of wine—that was unendurable.

CHAPTER FIVE

SOFIA was elated. After a bad beginning, things were going her way. Yesterday her father had thrashed her for wasting her time with a penniless holidaymaker, and although she had yelled and made a fuss, in a way she could not blame him. A girl must keep her eye on the main chance, and her main chance of getting away from Exos was as the wife of Marcus, who had money enough to buy a restaurant of his own.

True, it would be hard work, almost slavery. But at least one would be working for one's own home, husband, and children, not for some fat boss and his lazy fat wife. One would see life, meet new people every day, count the money every night.

It had been a bad error of judgment to overdo her attentions to the Irishman in her efforts to make Marcus jealous. She had frightened him off altogether. For two days he had not spoken to her, but gone fishing with her brothers or up the mountain by himself. She had nearly lost him, for a poverty-stricken tourist. Her father had been wise to take strong measures.

And now, everything was fine. The Kyrios McDermot had money. He intended to buy the big villa. Evie's mother had sent word to the go-between and the priest to begin talks about the price. That was an open secret already. Sofia's father had practically apologised for beating her, and her mother was already talking of having a daughter queening it up there on the hillside. For why—they asked themselves—should a stranger buy a house on such a small, unimportant island, if not because he intended to marry a local girl and settle down among his in-laws?

Now she would see the world at her ease, as a tourist herself. She would have a camera and sun-glasses, and laze on hotel beaches in a bikini, as the wife of a well-to-do European.

So she touched glasses with Rory, their faces close together, and his eyes smiled into hers over the wine. She still felt the pressure of his hand, where for a moment his arm had slipped round her waist. She sighed happily.

'You, man,' said Marcus heavily, 'get out. This is my girl.'

Rory looked up at the big man standing over him. To Sofia's disappointment he looked frightened; but then who wouldn't? That Marcus was such a coarse brute.

'I'm sorry, mate,' Rory said easily. 'We were only sharing a glass of wine. Sit down and have a drink.'

Marcus sat down. 'I'll finish the bottle. But you'll clear off, mister. I won't have strangers making up to my girl.'

'The idea!' Sofia tossed her head. 'I'm not your girl. I've better fish to fry than a cheap *taverna* proprietor who hasn't even got a *taverna*. You're just as rough-mannered as you were before you went away. Go away, and leave me to talk with my friends.'

Rory protested, 'But Marcus is your friend. You told me—'

She shrugged her plump creamy shoulders. 'That was a long time ago. I knew no better. He dazzled me, with his fancy clothes and tight shoes, and the money he was flashing. But I'm a serious girl, Rory, and I can see there's nothing behind the coloured suit and the pocketbook. Nothing for me.' She gave Marcus a contemptuous look. 'Please go away. I'm busy.'

The men exchanged a dismayed glance.

'Trick?' Marcus raised his well-marked eyebrows. 'Who's playing tricks, Mr. McDermot? You had me fooled. Well, if you're going to marry her, that's your good luck. But if you're not—' His big teak-coloured hand folded into a fist. 'You'd better be, that's all.'

Rory blenched. 'It's no trick, Marcus. I've no wish to marry Sofia. She's your girl.'

Sofia looked from one to the other, bewildered. 'What are you two talking about? Are you playing a trick on me, both of you? If so, it's not k-kind.' Tears flowed down her rosy face. The cherry-coloured kissable mouth drooped.

'Don't cry,' Rory said gently. He felt himself in a trap, either accidental or, perhaps, arranged by these two against himself. His mind worked quickly, but for the moment he saw no opening. He couldn't possibly marry Sofia.

'Sofia, please stop. Marcus and I were playing a little trick on you, that's all. He loves you, he wants you to marry him. He was pretending to scare me, and I was going to run away, with my tail between my legs, to make him look a hero for you. Forgive us.'

'I'll forgive you. I won't forgive him. He's nothing but a great lout. All he wants a woman for is work and bed. I wouldn't marry him if he were the last man on Exos! I want to marry you, and live in the Villa Julia and do nothing but embroidery.'

Sofia's tear-drenched eyes widened as the words poured out of her. Now she had given it all away, but perhaps no harm would be done. There came a moment when a man had to be told, straight.

Marcus swore. 'So that's how it is? You lied to me,

Irishman. You've talked to her about marriage. You must have done.'

Rory said desperately, 'Oh, for goodness' sake, Sofia, stop snivelling and listen. What's this about the villa?'

'You're going to buy it, everybody knows that. We all thought you hadn't a *mil* and now it turns out you're rich.'

Rory stood up and kicked his chair away. 'Marcus, come to the harbour with me. I think I can explain. She's given me a clue.'

"Too late for explaining. You'll marry her or there are two fists of mine that will make you do it, besides a dozen more pairs like them. Talking of houses to a woman, and then pretending it was all a game! I'm not so easily fooled as you think.'

'Yesterday, I swear, she was crazy for you, Marcus. Sofia, for pity's sake tell him that's true. But today there was some talk of my buying the villa, and the Kyria Julia sent Georgi to the priest and a relative called Stephanos with a letter asking them to represent her in any dealings with me. It came to nothing. The family decided not to sell after all. But I suppose the news travelled all over the island before sundown.'

Marcus scratched his head. 'It would. You think Sofia switched her affections to you because she thought you had money?'

'And perhaps would give her an easier life. Is that it, Sofia? You might as well tell the truth, because I don't intend to marry you in any case, fists or no fists. I know you love Marcus. I know you'd hate my kind of life and the kind of man I am. Marcus is your own kind, girl. Do have a bit of sense.'

She wiped her eyes and nose upon her apron. Rory grunted and handed her his handkerchief which had already had a hard day and was none too clean.

'You're all unkind to me! I'm going off with the

boat tomorrow. I'm a good waitress and I can get a job in Cyprus now the holiday season is on. I won't have anything to do with either of you. You're cruel!'

She spat on the ground, tossed her head, and flounced off, pushing her way through the crowd which had followed the quarrel with intense interest.

'Women!' groaned Marcus. 'Now where do we stand?'

'Keep after her,' Rory advised. 'She's a girl worth having. As for me, I'd better leave as soon as possible. I meant to stay a while in case—' he shot a glance in the direction of the Villa Julia, whose lights could be seen high on the dark hillside. 'But I'm not safe here, boy. When can I leave?'

Enquiries among the men sitting around revealed a small motor boat leaving about six in the morning. 'I'll go with that, if they'll have me,' Rory decided. 'Wait for the big caique at nine o'clock I dare not. Poor little Sofia is a woman scorned just now, and if I'm not careful she'll have the island knives out for me.'

'And you were the man who understood women!' Marcus mocked, not unkindly.

Evie spent a restless night. A vision of Rory and Sofia flashed across her mind and kept her wakeful. Heads close together, lips smiling over shared wine. Sofia, so vibrant, so alive and able to use her attractions to advantage. Evie had for some time been conscious that the girl she had grown up with was already fully occupied with the business of selecting and capturing the husband she wanted. Sofia seemed never to have known an in-between time, when she had stood with reluctant feet on the edge of growing-up, looking forward fearfully to the anxieties and bewilderment of being a young woman aware of herself, aware of young males. Lucky Sofia, to have such confidence in herself!

Sofia, if she had devised a plan for saving her home, would have carried it out with an air. I, Evie remembered wretchedly, felt sick with fear and ran away.

Perhaps Sofia had thought of a plan to get herself off Exos and out into the world? As Rory's wife! True, there was Marcus. But Sofia was shrewd enough to see that her future with Marcus would mean hard work and many children. Rory would be gentle with his wife, not demanding too much.

What if Rory married Sofia and brought her here, as mistress of the Villa Julia? Disturbed by the awful thought, Evie crept out of bed and to the verandah, where a cool air off the sea blew her thin cotton nightdress around her. The moon hung like a ripe peach in the sky, making a silver path across the still sea.

She closed her eyes tightly as if she could shut out the picture of Rory with Sofia. They still floated there, blobs of colour printed on her eyelids. Her attention sharpened suddenly, and she drew in a quick breath.

Had Marcus really been there, standing huge and still behind Rory, full of menace as he stared down at the Irishman's back? Or was Marcus only part of her dreams?

Didn't Rory McDermot know that, whatever the custom in his own country, in the Greek islands it was dangerous to play around with another man's girl? He must be warned.

With this thought uppermost in her mind, in the morning she hurried down to the village long before the caique was due to leave. She must find Rory and warn him. After their tumultuous parting of yesterday, their meeting might cause slight embarrassment on both sides, but that did not matter. There were men on the island capable of slipping a knife between the stranger's ribs. Not Marcus himself, perhaps, though he might use fists. The younger men were more travelled and better educated. But the older men, especially the grandfathers, still had ideas of an older and rougher justice.

The men were working in the fields, the harbour empty of boats except for the Kyrenia caique now being loaded. The wooden chairs of the *taverna* were stacked neatly outside, and Sofia herself was on hands and knees scrubbing the floor.

'Good morning, Sofia. How are your bruises?'

The girl wrung out her floorcloth. 'What bruises? Where are you going, all dressed up so early? If you've come to see Rory McDermot, you have wasted your breath. He's gone, left in a fishing boat before dawn.'

Relief flooded Evie's mind, till she thought of asking cautiously whose boat. An accident at sea would be convenient.

'Marcus and his father. They're taking him to Kyrenia. It seems he was in a hurry and couldn't wait for the caique. He won't be back. He took his backpack and everything from his room—not that he possessed much.'

Sofia was in a bad temper, that was obvious. Evie wasn't surprised. Scrubbing the *taverna* couldn't be pleasant, and if Rory had gone for good, after last night's little tender episode at the café table, Sofia must be feeling hurt and angry.

'What happened last night?' Evie asked gently. 'Did Rory quarrel with anyone?'

Sofia slapped her dirty cloth into the bucket. 'No, he did *not*. He and Marcus were as thick as thieves. I've finished with both of them, and I told them so. I gave them the length of my tongue, I can tell you. If either of them shows his face in this *taverna* again, I'll—I'll—oh, *go away!*'

Evie sat down on a dry piece of floor. This required investigation, and she understood very well that Sofia wanted to talk about it and was only letting off steam when she said *go away*. 'What did they do? Something terrible?'

'They were laughing at me, behind my back. I had a secret with Rory, and he told Marcus. And they tried to play a trick on me which didn't work, because I—I—'

Indignation gave way to a choking sob. The big dark eyes filled with tears, and Sofia looked at Evie with an expression of anguish.

'I love Marcus, Evie. Truly I do. But I hate scrubbing floors, and cooking, and if I marry him I'll never see anything any more but a kitchen stove and a tub of baby things to wash. What's the good of being pretty, and having nice clothes, and being the lightest dancer on the island, if it all leads to the washtub and the scrubbing brush? Isn't there anything else for us?'

'There's love.'

Sofia looked at her scornfully. 'Be your age, Evie! Love's a trap. We've no choice, really; only between scrubbing one's own floor and someone else's.'

Evie knew a piercing sense of desolation. 'But there must be more than that, Sofia. If I loved a man, I'd want to be with him for ever. I wouldn't care how hard life was, or mind working. Just so long as we were together.'

If I loved a man! I do. I love Rory and he's gone for ever. I'll never see him again. He won't come back, and it's partly my fault.

'You've grown up without a man in the house,' Sofia reminded her. 'You've had only yourselves to please, up there. No man coming in wanting food at all hours, with his tempers and tantrums and lazing about playing cards or drinking while his wife works herself to death. Men!' She threw the brush across the floor. 'I'd go into a convent, only—'

'Only what?'

Sofia shrugged. 'Well, I suppose one might miss something. And it wouldn't be much fun. You didn't tell me where you are going? Not Kyrenia?'

Evie nodded. 'On family business. And to buy some new dress materials. And I'd like my red shoes back, if you please.'

'I'll get them. Wait a minute.'

What's it all for? Sofia had asked of love. What indeed? Evie wondered, fingering the handmade lace collar on her clean black dress, the scarlet apron rich with embroidery, the white stockings she had washed last night and put on with pride this morning. Why bother to dress up? Much better to stick to old clothes which wouldn't spoil, and race about barefoot on the hottest days.

'Good morning, Evie.' The old priest paused in his shuffle down the waterfront. 'Going in the caique? You look too smart for Exos, so early. And deep in thought, eh? Dreaming of sweethearts to come?'

'Wishing time could stand still.'

'Dear child! When we wish that, it's already too late. You want it to stand still *yesterday*, don't you?'

'Yes, I do. Or better still, the day before yesterday.'

'You see? Too late already. I can't help you. Even the most powerful saints can't turn the clock back for us. I'm afraid we have to move forward into our own future all the time. Everything comes, if we wait long enough. And everything passes, even today's grief which seems so interminable. Well, have a good day, child. If you've time, call in and say a prayer with our dear St. Poly. He'll be glad to see someone from home, I daresay.'

'I intended to. I have a favour to ask him.'

'The saints, and God himself, would be lonely indeed if mankind wasn't always in need of a favour or two. Tell him the island needs him.'

Sofia came back with the shoes. The caique took on passengers and put out of the harbour. Evie settled down for a three-hour voyage, and composed her mind to deciding what exactly she would say to the lawyer.

Kyrenia was full of tourists. Like a walking flower-garden of colour, they wandered round the old harbour, climbed the great steps to the castle which had seen so many conquerors and conquered. Under coloured café-umbrellas they drank tea and studied their history books, or crowded round the water-ski boats. Evie walked up and down several times, carefully studying the dresses. Bright, bold colours looked best under the sun. Pastel colours appeared faded against the vivid sea and sky. She studied the blonde girls of her own age with particular interest, even following one group as far as the foot of the castle steps to observe the details; but then she realised her time was flying and she must find the lawyer's office before it closed for the long lunch period.

The lawyer, who was younger and less dusty than she'd expected, listened attentively. He wouldn't guarantee results, but he would try through English agents. Perhaps it would be best to advertise in the English national newspapers. Would that be in order?

'Whatever you think best,' Evie told him. 'How long will it take?'

'To put the advertisements in, only a week, perhaps. But don't expect too much. After so many years, it will be difficult. Perhaps impossible.'

'I understand that,' Evie assured him. 'But at least we shall have tried.'

Leaving him, she decided to visit St. Polystemon

next, leaving her shopping till the late afternoon so that she could take her parcels direct to the boat. She put the red shoes carefully into her shabby shoulder-bag, donned her old sandals and began the long trudge uphill towards the tiny monastery which had the honour of sheltering the saint's skull. She could eat her fruit lunch by the roadside and with luck she would be offered a lift.

Her luck held. An old man stopped his donkey cart and courteously offered her his hospitality. She shared her lunch with him and told him about St. Polystemon, and Exos. When they parted he kissed her ceremoniously on both cheeks and gave her his blessing. Ten minutes' scrambling up a steep path brought her to the old buildings and she was thankful to rest in the shady cloisters to recover her breath.

All was silent. A cat slept in the sun. The heat brought out the scent of herbs growing in red pots on top of a wall. Four tall cypresses stood like dark motionless sentries, and not even a leaf quivered in the still air.

The interior of the chapel was dark after the sunlight. Only the gold paint of the icons, and the high gilded candleholders, gleamed dimly. Evie sat on a wooden narrow seat till her eyes adjusted to the gloom.

She found St. Polystemon's skull in a blackened case in the darkest corner. Disappointed, for she had always been told it was in a silver box, she peered closely and found a hole in the case, through which a tiny circle of bone shone, polished by generations of hopeful fingers. Closing her eyes, she concentrated her whole mind upon a fervent prayer to the young saint.

Please, oh, please bring Rory McDermot back! I want him so much.

She opened her eyes, knowing she had wasted her effort after all. She had meant to ask for her father to be found. Now she could see much better, and observed that the case really was silver after all; but it had not been polished for many years. Now if the monks had a woman about the place, to do the cleaning and such, poor St. Poly would not be so neglected. Well, it was something to tell them at home, and perhaps stop them asking what she had prayed for.

It isn't, the old priest had told her often enough, that the saints really do interfere with our lives down here; but praying so hard, and meaning it, helps us to know what it is we *really* want. Which isn't always just what we think we want.

She smiled ruefully. Well, at least St. Poly might be glad to know he wasn't forgotten in Exos, poor young man. How sad it must be, to lose bright life at twenty years old, for the sake of an ideal! She stooped and dropped a kiss on the polished ivory bone, and whispered the priest's message.

Then she went outside, into the sun and blinking like a little owl. St. Polystemon had done his work well, for there, coming under the archway, his pack on his back, was Rory.

They stared at each other, unbelieving. Then she ran towards him and was snatched up into his arms. He hugged her tightly.

'Evie! Darling girl, what on earth are you doing so far from home? Of all people—?'

'I'm visiting St. Poly, of course. Do you think I'd come this far, and not pay my respects? But—oh, Rory, I thought you'd gone for ever! How come you are here? Did you know about me?'

'No. I just walked up, by the footpath. After my stay in Exos, it seemed the right thing to do—as you said, to pay my respects.'

There was, after all, no awkwardness. Only a bubbling delight at being with him again, a delight he obviously shared.

'Show me your saint, then we'll walk down the hill together and have tea at the hotel on the beach. A civilised tea, which Cyprus understands, thank goodness. There's a lovely path all the way down and we shall have a fine thirst at the end of it.'

'I have shopping to do, and the caique leaves before dark. Are you coming back to Exos? Sofia says you took all your things away.'

Not till they were on the downhill path did he tell her why he had left the island so early. 'I ran away. Somehow the news of my trying to buy the villa got out. And Marcus and I burned our fingers trying to be too clever with Sofia. She suddenly decided she wanted to marry me instead of him, and when she understood that wasn't the idea, she was angry with both of us. What could I do but run? With me out of the way, she may forgive poor Marcus in time. I'm afraid it was all my doing.'

'When I saw you last night, you were making silly eyes at her over a wineglass. And Marcus—' she stopped suddenly. 'Then he *was* there, behind you! Don't you know how dangerous it is to play around with another man's girl? He could have killed you. I remembered in the night that he was there, and I was so afraid for you, Rory. I had to go down to warn you early this morning; but you'd gone.'

'That was darned nice of you, Evie. I thought you'd finished with me for ever, and I was sorry about that. Much as I wanted the villa, it suddenly seemed to me that I didn't want to quarrel with you over it, so I decided to give up the idea of buying it. Does that solve your problem?'

They had arrived at a flat little clearing and sat down by mutual consent, as from it there was a splendid view down into the inner courts of the castle where once

Crusaders had walked, and where now coloured dots of sightseers moved like insects. Beyond the huge bastion of grey stone the sea shimmered like silk, and water-skiers carved long arcs of white upon the blue. The bank on which they sat was covered in creamy rock-roses which smelt delicious.

'Not exactly,' Evie admitted. 'Mama won't give up the idea of selling, and if it is not you, it might be someone much worse.'

'Thank you.'

'Well, there could be worse than you. If you married Sofia and made her mistress of the house, that would be the worst thing of all.'

'My dear child, I have no intention of marrying Sofia and never have had. Whatever made you think so?'

'She's so pretty. I'm not in the least like her.'

'No, you're not in the least like Sofia.'

'I'm not pretty?'

'No, you're not pretty.'

'Sofia attracts all the men, without even trying. I can't do that.'

'No, you can't.'

'Anybody could be in love with Sofia.'

He twisted to face her, and took both her narrow tanned hands in his. 'Listen, dear Evie. You are not pretty like Sofia because you are beautiful. You have lovely bones and an elegant walk like a queen's; and this beauty you will keep. When Sofia is a fat momma waddling about her work, you will be beautiful still. When you are an old, old lady, you will be as fine and delicate as hand-made lace.'

'Rory—'

'Sofia is young enough to attract all men. She attracts me, in her way. But you, my sweet, will draw one man to you, and pierce him to the bone with love.

And he will love you the whole of his lone life, and beyond the grave itself. You have the power, mavourneen, which one woman in a million possesses. Do you understand?'

She shook her head. 'Not entirely. You bewilder me, Rory.'

He cupped her face between his hands, 'Some day—soon—you'll know what I mean. Meantime, don't compare yourself with Sofia. She's pretty, she's vividly alive, she could win any man's body. Yes, mine too, if she tried and I were not obsessed with another woman. But you, my sweet, will win a man's soul and keep it.'

She did not answer because there were no words. She stared down into her hands, and felt the warm air moving round her, and inhaled the scent of the rock roses and heard a bee. She thought, When I am very old, I shall remember this minute of my life.

After a bit, she remembered something he had said. 'Obsessed with another woman? You mean—there's someone you want to marry?'

He smiled and shook his head. 'Wanted. She married another man. I can't get her out of my head. Not yet. It's too soon.'

'She pierced you to the bone?'

'It wasn't like that. We grew up together. We were like twins, happier together than with anyone else. We thought each other's thoughts. I never dreamed either of us could think of marrying anyone else. There was no one I was more content to be with.'

'And she with you?'

'I thought so.'

She said carefully, 'It seems to me you were good, close friends. Isn't love something different again? You could quarrel every day with someone, and yet be in love.'

98

He stabbed at the dry soil with a broken-off stick. 'It could be. Do you know, we never had any need to talk, Clodagh and I.'

'Maybe you had nothing to say to each other.'

He gave her an odd look. 'I'd have walked off and left you on your lee lone if you'd dared say that six months ago. Silent companionship, we used to call it. And I daresay it was, most of the time. Lately I've wondered if we'd exhausted all we had to talk about. A lifetime of it might have proved lonely, to say the least.'

'One day you'll wake up and find yourself free of her. I feel it in my bones. Then you'll want another girl.'

'I shall never be quite free of Clodagh. She's part of me, like the sea breaking on the Irish cliffs, and the bare white rocks, and cream-coloured Connemara ponies, and the scent of my country.' He laughed suddenly. 'You couldn't imagine how it smells, Evie. Rotting seaweed in the fields, and the smoke of burning turf from the house fires. And there are the finest horses and dogs in the world there. Times, the sea is as blue as the Mediterranean, but there are tides, and long white combers rolling in on the Atlantic beaches—'

'You love it, Rory? Why do you want a house here?'

'Because any house I had on the cliffs there would be Clodagh's house, don't you see? A white house on a cliff at the edge of the sea, that's what I always dreamed of. I can have it here, and the warmth of the sun beside, and the scent of lemons and lilies, balsam and basil, figs and wine.'

He lay flat on his back, hands under head, and stared unblinking at the sky. 'All over the world, girl, there are men like me; the lonely sort, whose dream is out of reach and can't be replaced by any everyday sort of girl. Men who, for a month or a year or for ever, want to be alone and not bothered by anyone. We are usually poor, mavourneen, because we have no incentive to keep on the roundabout of money, or to run in the rat race. Our links with life are broken and for a time we want to form no new ones.'

Evie stroked his forehead gently, aching with love.

'So when my old da died and left me all he had, which, God rest him, wasn't all that much, I dreamed up a house where such men might stay for a time in their aimless wandering. A healing place, with no ties to it. Where a man could come and go as he pleased, live on what he possessed in a simple sort of way; enjoy the sun and warmth, find a sort of medicine in the earth. Am I talking nonsense?'

'It sounds sensible to me. You think the Villa Julia might be such a place? There is space, and we grow things. The rooms are big and look out on the sea. But, Rory, think. It would never do. You mean a sort of hotel, don't you? There is only one bathroom, and the water has to be carried.'

'Then we should carry it, or wash in the stream. Or go unwashed, if we fancied. But we'd be no hippies, Evie. I don't mean that sort.'

'Sheets and tablecloths to be washed. You're not at all practical, my dear man. How would you cook meals for a lot of hungry men in my kitchen?'

'I wouldn't. There's an oven out in the yard, isn't there? They say bread and meat baked in those outdoor ovens taste wonderful. My guests would be content with that, and with honey and dates and grapes.'

She laughed softly. 'And pull faces over our goats milk? And goat cheese is strong.'

'All the better. But—' he sat up and collected his backpack, 'that's a dream from which I woke up pretty smartish yesterday. It wouldn't have worked, perhaps.'

'Monasteries work. Look at our Brothers. I don't see

why it shouldn't, except, of course, that it might be difficult to find the right people.'

'I don't think so. There's a grapevine among such men. I know, I'm one of them'

'Would you admit women?'

'Why not, if they had the need of such a retreat?'

'And everybody would be free to go back into the world as soon as they were ready to face it? It's a wonderful idea, Rory. Our house and our island working a cure on human hearts. I'd like that. Couldn't we do it without selling you the house? If you planned it all, and Mama and I helped with the housekeeping part of it?' Her voice lifted with enthusiasm as the future took shape in her mind. 'Mama and I could live in the village and come up every day, so you'd have our rooms for your guests. And we could keep the land for Georgi, and—'

He interrupted sharply. 'Forget it. It can't be done that way. Your mother wants the money—needs it. Your way, she'd get nothing for the house, for I wasn't thinking of making a profit, but only enough to pay my way and keep the place in repair. You wouldn't even get any wages, for my idea is that we look after ourselves, doing the cleaning and cooking, and growing our own food, doing our own fishing. You see, the place would have to be mine. No woman would go along with my simple ideas. You all want to dress things up, and none of you believes that a lonely man prefers to look after himself. You'd want clean table-cloths instead of scrubbed board; and regular meal times, and before long you'd be laundering our shirts. I know women! They interfere.'

'Mama might. She'd fuss and worry. But I'd never interfere, only help.'

'And be hurt if I told you to clear off when I didn't want any help!'

The words came harshly, and almost at once he stood up and hitched his pack on his shoulders. 'It wouldn't work, Evie. That's not the way I dreamed it. I can't have my idea cluttered up with a lot of women fussing around. Come on, if you want that tea and to do your shopping. I'll put you on the evening boat, but I'm not coming back to Exos. I'll find my house somewhere else.'

Tears stung her eyes, but she blinked them back, too proud to let him see he had hurt her. She sprang to her feet.

'Come on, then. I'll race you down the hill.' She sped away, her feet light on the steep track. The path was more fitted for goats than human beings, and, more accustomed than he to such walking, she came first to the road and waited for him.

This was the last time, then. After today Rory would be gone out of her life. The thought was anguish and she closed her eyes, trying to fix these final moments in her memory for ever. The heat beating on her face, the smell of crushed herbs, the sound of his feet on the stones. She made herself open her eyes to look up to see him, tall and lean, silhouetted against the brilliant sky. The shape of his head, the shape of his ears, the easy way his muscles moved, the shabby blue shirt and strong brown arms. When he has gone, she thought, I might just as well stop breathing.

Rory, clattering down the steep track, was smitten with remorse at the hard way he'd refused her offer of help. Why, in the name of the saints, couldn't he have said at least a thank-you? She'd understood what he was about, and women so rarely did. He believed her when she said she wouldn't interfere. She was nobody's fool, that girl; yet she had a kind of simple humility, a refreshing lack of complication, which he had known sometimes in the older generation of Irish women. It came, perhaps, from living hand in glove with saints and close to the earth and sea. In her beauty there was the same serenity he remembered in the face of his grandmother. Dammit, why did he have to hurt her?

When he stood beside her, he took her hand lightly in his. 'Forgive my abominable manners,' he said quietly. 'That was a kind thought of yours, and if anyone could make it work, you could.'

She turned her head away, afraid he would read too much in her face. 'It doesn't matter. You were right. Mama needs the money, and I do understand that the house would have to be your own so you could have everything your way. Forget about it.'

'Look at me, Evie.'

Reluctantly she obeyed, lifting her face to his. His eyes were intent and grave, so close that she could see her reflection in his pupils. 'I hurt you, when you only meant to help. That was inexcusable of me. Believe me, it means a lot to me that you understand me. No one else has, in quite the same way. I shall not forget you, Evie, not ever, wherever I go. Maybe I'm a fool to go at all, but I'd be no good to you. My dream is in me, and I can't settle until I find it. But I'll always know there was one girl who understood how it is with me.'

She nodded seriously. 'I think I do. I think my father was the same. He had to go, you see. The island could not hold him because there was other music in his ears. So he left my mother and I don't think he'll ever come back. If there's a bit of him in me, that's the bit which understands you.'

He leaned nearer, and kissed her softly on the lips— a kiss as light as a butterfly's touch, the first she had ever known from a young man, and like no other kiss she had ever experienced. Her pulses raced, the quick response of her body startled her and she gave a soft cry almost of pain. Before she could move, he pulled her into his arms and kissed her again more closely, his mouth hard on hers.

Terrified, not of him but of her own body, she struggled to be free. He released her suddenly, sensing her terror and remembering the feel of a small wild creature in his hands.

She stared at him wide-eyed. 'What have you done to me? What have you done?'

He drew a deep breath through his nostrils. He could have kicked himself for being so stupid! He might have known the girl had never been kissed before, and was not for casual kissing like any ordinary girl. He had intruded most damnably into the secret places of her being, and should have had the sense to hold back. He had meant the kiss only in the way of friendship and as a token of remembrance; why did he have to follow it up with the second one, which young Sofia, that hibiscus flower open to the sun, would have accepted with a laugh and returned with delight?

'Nothing at all,' he said gently, as he would reassure a frightened animal. 'Just a kiss in friendship, Evie. A thank-you for understanding me. Don't think any more about it.'

She would. And he would, too. *What have you done to me?* she had asked. What have I done to myself? he wondered. Why, suddenly, do I feel we belong together, the way I felt with Clodagh?

He tucked her arm in his and marched her down the road. 'I promised you tea, my girl, and we're going to the best hotel I can find, by way of a goodbye party. We shall gorge ourselves with honey and almond cakes, and chocolate ice-creams if there's such a thing to be had.'

She did not answer, did not look at him. But she accepted his arm in hers, and marched heel-and-toe with him on the dusty road. Give her time, he thought.

A little time to recover herself and no harm will be done. Only the first kiss has gone, never to return; and that she needed, to save for the lad who will marry her.

That thought had twisted like a knife. What rough male would handle this soft-mouthed, delicate-stepping thoroughbred, break the gentle proud spirit to bridle and rein? He had suffered much, thinking of fine Clodagh in the hands of the Englishman from Somerset, though Clodagh herself seemed happy enough. Was he to suffer again, remembering the silvery girl he had left on Exos, and for ever wondering who? And how?

They came to the hotel. Evie stared at the flower-hung entrance, the swinging doors of plate-glass, the tourists strolling in and out.

'I can't go in there, Rory. I'm not dressed for a place like this. Only my black dress and apron—it isn't fitting.'

'Nonsense! You're more beautiful than any of these globe-trotting old dears. They'll envy you your hair, your face and your mouth. They'll tell all their friends at home about the lovely island girl in her embroidered apron and lace cap, and feel they've been privileged to look at you. You're your father's daughter, my lass, and twice as good as anyone here. Come on.'

She hung back. 'Wait a minute. I've clean stockings and my red shoes in the bag. Let me put them on.'

She spent a long time in the cloakroom, enjoying the row of pink washbasins, the shining taps which gave hot water, the scented soap. There was a towel, snowy-white but too short to use. When she pulled it in exasperation, it startled her by coming out of its white box, seemingly endless, and refusing to be rolled back. Washed and tidied, and in her red shoes, she stared at herself in the long looking-glass which reflected her image over and over again, and touched her mouth wonderingly.

Why, oh, why did he kiss me? It makes it so much harder to forget that I love him.

My father's daughter? She looked more closely at herself. Am I like him? What sort of man was he, my father? I don't really remember him; only what my mother tells me about him, and that isn't the same.

She remembered she had not told Rory about her visit to the lawyer. Well, that was not his affair. He would hardly be interested, as he was leaving Exos and had given up the idea of buying the villa. It was not polite to thrust one's own domestic affairs before other people who could not possibly be interested.

Leaving the luxurious cloakroom with a certain reluctance, she held her head high and walked out to meet Rory, not noticing the admiring glances cast in her direction by the discreet parties of hotel guests gathering in the vast cool marble-floored lounge for an English-style afternoon tea.

Rory noticed—and smiled to himself. How easily this girl could adapt to a more civilised background than the island afforded! With the right man to guide her gently along the right lines, she could fit into a new life with natural grace and easy charm. She had the looks, the education, the unaffected manner of a great lady. Surely fate did not intend her to become a village drudge, blowsy and shrewish as so many peasant women became after a few years? If the father came back, he might be the sort of man who could give his daughter a chance.

A white-coated waiter brought tea. Evie poured out, her fine hands delicate among the china and silver. There was a subdued murmur of English voices, a tinkle of water in a marble fountain. Beyond the wide windows, a flash of brilliant turquoise was the swimming-pool, edged by flowering plants and palms.

Evie sighed. 'It's very *rich*, isn't it? I mean, everything must cost such a lot. I'd like to live here for a week. It would take me all that long, just to try everything and see how it worked. Pink tablecloths, too. Oh, look, there's a glass case of embroidery. Is it all right to go and have a look?'

'That's why it is there.'

She examined the display carefully, and came back to him simmering with anger. 'That big cloth is Mama's work. It is priced at one hundred pounds. That's sinful! Mama gets no more than twenty, yet it is the best piece of work there. I don't say that because it is my mama's, but because it really is.'

'Then you've learned something today. Your mama must ask more for her work.'

She was disturbed by the discovery. 'A hundred pounds! How can people pay so much? How much will this tea cost you?'

Seeing she was serious he told her, adding, 'Don't worry! I can afford it.'

She shook her head crossly. 'We are spending on one meal enough to keep an island family for half a month. Yet there's not much food. It's all the—' she gestured vaguely, 'all the pretty surroundings. Big comfortable chairs, and soft rugs, and flowers everywhere—and music. How much will you tip the waiter?'

'Ten per cent.'

She worked it out, and nodded with satisfaction. 'Yes, I see now why all the boys want to leave Exos to be waiters. Is there also ten per cent for a waitress? Perhaps I could be one, when Sofia leaves. We could go together, and earn a lot. Then I could help Mama.'

'No,' he said sharply. 'No, Evie. It is no life for you. For Sofia it's all right. Not you.'

'Why not me? I'm very strong, in spite of being so skinny.'

'Your father would not like it. I mean—well, I wouldn't like it.'

She bubbled with soft laughter. 'But, Rory, you are not my father.'

'Sometimes I feel old enough to be. But I'm glad I'm not.'

Her eyes twinkled mischievously at him. 'If you were, you'd beat me, eh?'

'Certainly I would.'

It seemed the right moment to tell Rory of her visit to the lawyer, and the advertisements which were to be inserted in English newspapers, but just then a bevy of girls of her own age trooped in, laughing and chattering, and it was necessary to examine their dresses carefully.

'Which one is for me?' she wondered. 'I can't go about in an old peasant gown any more.'

'The blue,' he answered without hesitation. 'The style is simple enough, but I doubt if you'd buy one here in Kyrenia. The girls are American.' He pulled out a pencil and sketched a dress on the back of a menu card.

'Mama can make it. She's clever with sewing. Draw some more, Rory. Please. And will you help me choose some material? You know about what looks elegant, don't you?'

He laughed. 'Since when did our tomboy wish to look elegant? Are you growing up, acushla?'

'I have to. So I might as well do it properly. Will you come? Had you planned to do anything else? Where are you going, after today?'

'I've no plans, except that it would be fun to spend the rest of the day with you. Now we've stopped quarrelling about the house, we get on pretty well, don't you think?'

'I'm glad you think so. Rory, I'm happy *now*. At this

moment in my life. If all the rest of it were to be unhappy, I'd have this minute to remember, wouldn't I? So I intend to enjoy it to the very end. Ought we to go now? The shops will be open again. It's quite late.'

The shops were opening after the long midday break. Holidaymakers were out again, now the afternoon was somewhat cooler. 'You must visit the castle,' she told him helpfully, 'but not till tomorrow because it takes ages and is tiring. Will this shop do? The prices seem reasonable.'

He dismissed the shop as too cheap and walked her through the town till he found one to his liking. 'In here, and I'll choose.'

Meekly, she trotted in after him, but gasped with dismay at the price of the dress-lengths he indicated. 'No one in Exos pays that much.'

'But you will. You're a special case. Remember, Evie, you must always buy things of quality, because you are a quality person yourself. Look, this is your colour. It will match your eyes.'

The soft folds of fine cotton fell through her fingers. 'It is the colour of the sea. It will look beautiful, Rory.'

'And this one.'

She looked doubtfully at the bold, dark design. 'Are you sure? Not the pink?'

'Definitely not the pink. Trust me. I know about colours. Your friend Sofia would buy this and look ghastly in it. You will look superb. And while you are here, if you can afford it, buy yourself some good shoes.'

'I have good shoes. The red ones.'

He shook his head, smiling.

Her eyes widened. 'They look ghastly?'

'Terrible. I prefer your sandals any day.'

She flashed him a grin. 'So do I. But nobody else on Exos has red shoes and I thought maybe I was a bit peculiar, not liking them. I made myself like them, and in the end I did. Is it all right to wear sandals again now?'

'Please do.'

To the amusement of the shop assistant, Evie at once whipped off the red shoes, which were making her feet ache, and wriggled her toes ecstatically. Then she put on the old sandals with relief, and considered the question of paying for the materials Rory had chosen.

'Mama said I'd need three dresses, one for Sundays and church, one for everyday and one for going out in the evenings. But I can only manage two at these prices. Perhaps—' her glance strayed towards the pile of cheap stuff on the bargain counter.

'Don't compromise. Take two and wear your old black for every day. And let me buy you the shoes as a thank-you present.'

'Thank-you what for? Sending you to the copper-mines on a donkey?'

'For today. For you to remember today.'

She looked up at him seriously. 'I shan't forget today, Rory. Never fear, I'll tell Mama I bought shoes instead of the third dress. She'd never approve of a man buying me presents to wear. Only a husband does that.' Her colour deepened suddenly. 'Whenever we get together, I tell lies. Is it dreadful of me to lie to Mama? I could manage without the shoes.'

'Just this once,' he assured her, 'I'll overlook it. I am, thank God, not your father.'

The shopping done, they strolled to the waterfront. The island men were loading the caique, but there was plenty of time, Rory pointed out, for a glass of *ouzo* before it sailed. He found a pleasant *taverna* with basket chairs and tables on the street, and ordered.

They sat in silence, staring at the red marker buoys floating in the harbour.

Rory thought about Clodagh. Today had been a day very like one spent with Clodagh; a happy, untroubled day, warm with the closeness of a person who understood one's inner thoughts and with whom there was no need to pretend. He tried to fix his mind on the Irish girl, but her image was elusive. Am I forgetting her? he thought with alarm. I cannot forget her. She is part of me; without her, I am always incomplete. I *can't* forget Clodagh.

Yet it seemed to him his childhood sweetheart was drifting into a faint formlessness, like the vanishing of a smoke ring. And here, beside him, was Evie, warm and living; a creature of earth and air and fire, with whom a man might fall in love so easily, and stay in love for ever.

His throat burned drily. By the saints, he thought suddenly shaken—it's not Sofia I'm running away from, at all. It's her—Evie. Because I'm so darned nearly in love with her that I'm jealous for Clodagh.

He remembered the way Evie had looked up at him so seriously, and said in her soft musical voice *I shan't forget today, Rory, never fear*. He mopped his forehead with his handkerchief and a faint groan escaped him.

Evie was clasping her hands, shaking with nerves now the moment had come. Yesterday she had shirked it and was ashamed of her cowardice. Now time was running out. In fifteen minutes the caique would leave, taking her back to Exos, leaving Rory here on the harbour wall. So little time in which to keep her promise to her young brother. *I'll do everything in my power*, she had sworn, and Georgi trusted her. True, she had put the matter of tracing their father in hand, but the lawyer had held out little hope.

She cleared her throat, swallowed, and turned to him, her eyes big with the enormity of what she was about to say.

'Rory, there is a solution. A way you could buy the house from Mama, and yet not take it away from us entirely. I mean, you'd be master of the house because it would be yours, and yet—' she paused, licking dry lips. She could not go on.

His dark brows lifted. 'By magic, acushla? The house to be mine and yet yours? How?'

She went on hurriedly, 'I'd help, I really would. And so would Georgi. He's useful on the land, even at his age, and Mama would be quite happy to live in her own little house, and—'

He laid a strong hand on her arm. 'Steady, girl. Take a deep breath and tell me slowly. What are you driving at?'

She looked him full in the face, meeeting his questioning gaze without fear now. 'There's only one way to do it, Rory. I thought—perhaps—do you think you could marry me?'

CHAPTER SIX

RORY sat stunned in silence, staring at the toes of his dusty shoes on the blue-grey cobblestones of Kyrenia waterfront. Words rose in his throat and died.

He had enough peasant blood in him, from his Irish ancestors, to understand that such an arrangement had merits and would be accepted by Kyria Julia and her advisers without surprise. It would solve many problems. It meant, simply, that the daughter's children inherited and not the son's. The family was indivisible, so the land would not be divided. From a practical point of view, Evie's astonishing proposal was a good one.

He was more than half in love with her, and Clodagh had gone out of his life forever. Evie would be a good, obedient wife, run his home excellently, take care of his creature comforts and make no unreasonable demands on him. From his angle, it was a good bargain, since there would never be a great love in his life again and on the whole a man is more comfortable married than not.

'It wouldn't be fair to you,' he said at last, in a croaking voice. 'I'm seven years older than you, Evie. Seven bruising years which have taken some of the youth out of me. You need someone young and untiring, with laughter in his mouth and not afraid of the future.' He put an arm round her shoulder. 'Believe me, dear, *dear* Evie, you have paid me the great compliment of my life, which I shall never forget even when I'm so old that I've forgotten everything else. But it wouldn't do, dear heart. You must see more of the world, more of men and women. You've had no chance yet, to know people of your own sort.'

'I know you. I don't want to meet a lot of people, and if I did, I'd still like you best and want to marry you.'

'Marriage lasts a long time. Have you the least idea what it means?'

Flushing, she turned away. 'I'm not an ignorant child. My mother has trained me well. I'd make a good wife, I think. But please forget I asked. If I don't please you in that way, there's no more to be said. I only thought that since you can't marry *her*, it wouldn't make all that difference who you married. I could be useful to you, and it would settle the problems about the house. Only I see it won't do. You're still too much in love with her, aren't you?'

Evie wished she were a million miles away. She had made her supreme effort and failed. Now she wanted only to hide her humiliation from him, and the minutes before the caique was due to sail stretched out like a whole day.

She had not told him she loved him. That she would never do, until he loved her. A business proposition was a sensible enough thing to make; a declaration of love was something different, and must wait for its proper time. And that time, she knew in her bones, would never come now.

'You please me enormously, Evie. It's just that I couldn't bring myself to take advantage of your inexperience. I've practically no money. I earn a modest amount by writing, but I'll never be comfortably off and my wife would have to scrape by on very little. That's not for you. You are a jewel worthy of a splendid setting—clothes, luxury, travel, all the things a beautiful woman should have by right. Such a chance may come your way soon and I won't let you tie yourself up to a vagabond while you're still in your teens. It wouldn't be right.'

She nodded sadly. 'I must go. The men are ready to sail. We must say goodbye now, Rory. But if you change your mind, I shan't change mine. I don't say things lightly and I really meant it. Come to the island any time, if you think my solution would work. You may, when you've had time to think it over. Goodbye now.'

He lifted her hand and touched it with his lips. 'Bless you, Princess. Think kindly of me if you can, and forgive me. I'll never forget the honour you've done me—never.' His face was bleak, the high cheekbones showing pale against the dark-tanned skin. There was a lump in his throat that needed swallowing.

He watched the blue and orange painted caique out of the harbour, and stayed there, staring out to sea, till the swift Mediterranean night came down, like a curtain of violet silk over the end of the day; and the stars shone silver.

'Rory McDermot,' he told himself at long last, 'you are the fool of all the world. There goes a girl in a million, and you have shamed her in her own sight. A decent man would kick you from here to the top of the Troodos mountains.'

He sighed, shouldered his pack again and set off to walk. The top of the Troodos mountains was as good a place as any, and to get there on his two feet would give him plenty of time for thinking.

When the boat was clear of the harbour, Evie's second cousin Andreas, who was one of the vessel's joint owners, came and sat beside her. 'Wasn't that the man who is going to buy your mother's house? They say he's enormously wealthy and will bring tourists by the hundred to Exos.'

'He's not and he won't. The deal is off. That man hasn't the money that will buy our house, and who wants tourists? They spoil a place.'

'The men don't say so. We want tourists. They bring money with them, and why should Exos be left out when there's prosperity flying around? We heard he was going to build a big hotel up there, with a swimming pool. We were considering buying a new boat. This old hulk won't serve the island much longer, and a boat this size costs real money. Your mother wanted to sell, right enough. She sent to the priest and Uncle Stephanos, to act as go-betweens. So why is it off, now? Is it your doing? If so, you won't be popular on Exos. We all want change. You'd better get him back, if you're the one who sent him away.'

She was nearly dropping with fatigue and lost in unhappiness, but when the sense of what Andreas was saying penetrated, she was furiously angry.

'So? We sell our home, our land, for the sake of everybody else on the island? You're all going to get rich, are you, when we are homeless and Georgi has lost his heritage for ever? Why don't you sell your own houses, your own lemon groves? Sell the boat—why not? Because it's your livelihood? But you'd be happy to see my mother sell ours. The land is rightly my brother's. Tell that to your friends when you're drinking *ouzo* tonight.'

'All right, don't bite my head off. I'm only telling you what everybody is saying. News travels fast, as you well know. There isn't a family on the island but is looking forward to money flowing in.'

'Pass this news round, then. There isn't to be a hotel. There never was. Swimming pool, tourists, the lot. It's all grown out of your own highly spiced imaginations and too much *ouzo*. He wanted the house for himself and a few friends with as little money as himself, that's all.'

She turned away and hunched up into a shawl she had brought for the journey. The sea breeze was cool, now the sun had gone.

Andreas massaged his head. 'It was all a rumour?' He laughed suddenly and slapped his knee. 'That's Exos for you! A man has only to scratch his land with a broken stick and his neighbours are harvesting next year's grapefruit for him.'

To Evie's relief, he lost interest and left her. Or maybe he went to break the news to his partners that the old boat would have to serve a few more years. She rested her head against a wooden block, hearing the creaking of the ancient timbers and the hiss of the sea, the hard smack of the sail in the wind. She closed her eyes, and let quiet tears ooze out under the lids. How tired she was, how exhausted.

She had yet to explain to her mother that the Kyrios McDermot had gone and would not be back. And Sofia would drill a confused story into her ears, about Marcus and Rory. The instalments of that might go on for weeks, unless Marcus shut her mouth by marrying her.

It had been a wonderful day. There would be no more like it.

Evie took up the threads of her everyday life again. A stranger had come and gone, that was all. That he had taken her heart with him, that she lived now with a painful emptiness where that heart used to be, hardly seemed to matter. There were the goats, the lemons to be harvested in due course; the dates to be netted; water to be dragged to the vegetable plot.

Her mother wept and scolded at the loss of a buyer. 'It is your fault, child. You were so rude to him, so unkind. How shall I face my husband, your father, now? His son an uncouth islander, uneducated?'

'Georgi is neither uneducated nor uncouth. He's good-mannered and thoughtful, and willing to work to keep his mother and sister. You ought to be thankful for him, Mama, and appreciate him as he is. You are looking for the golden apples of the Hesperides instead of enjoying the plain good fruit that grows in our own soil.'

'How dare you speak to your mother so? You are getting beyond control. I shall have to ask your uncle to thrash you, if you are so impudent.'

'Do that, and I shan't be here to receive the beating. I'm not a child to be rebuked, Mama. I can lead my own life and earn a living on the mainland, remember.'

When her anger cooled she felt sorry for having made her mother cry. A daughter shouldn't do that. A mother suffers enough for her children without their being ungrateful and rude besides. She apologised.

'I forgive you, Evie. You are right, I treat you as a baby still, when you are a woman. Look, I've finished the first dress, the blue one. See if you like it.'

'It will do,' Evie said indifferently. What use were new clothes now? Then, seeing the tears spring again to Julia's eyes, she tried the dress on and exclaimed with pleasure over the clever way her mother had reproduced the garment Rory had sketched, and the fine stitching.

'I'm lucky to have such a mother,' she said with real warmth, and hugged Julia till she protested that she could not breathe.

The girl spent more and more time up at the ruined temple, among her childhood friends the splendid headless statues of the gods. All she wanted was solitude, where she could live over and over again the moments with Rory. She held long conversations with him, but as she had to provide both sides of the talk, they were never satisfying.

Common sense told her to lose herself in work or study. Only occupation would give her a chance of forgetting the man who had taken her heart.

During the hot summer nights, Rory haunted her sleep. His thin brown face, the smiling blue eyes; the mouth that could be so grave, yet could twist into a mocking half smile. In her dreams that warm mouth kissed her many times. Many times she woke from such a dream to shed bitter tears.

There came no word at all from the lawyer, and as the weeks of summer passed the hope of hearing from him slowly died.

Marcus and Sofia were to be married. Sofia toiled up the hill in the heat to beg the loan of Julia's bridal crown.

'Everybody says it was the most beautiful they ever remember, kyria. And,' the flushed, excited bride-to-be glanced at Evie, 'it isn't as if you'll be wanting it for a long time. Who is there for poor Evie to marry?'

'But you said you didn't want to marry Marcus,' Evie reminded her when they were going down to the village, the precious bridal crown carefully wrapped in a white cloth. 'You said there'd be nothing but babies and scrubbing, and that marriage was a trap.'

Sofia gave her a patronising look. 'How little you know, Evie! Wait till a man asks you to marry him, then you'll understand. It's a pity you didn't try for that Irishman who was here. He wasn't much, and poor as a priest, but at least he was a man and would have given you children. I never did believe that ridiculous story that he meant to buy your house. He hadn't two *mils* in his pocket.'

'Then why should I marry him?' Evie said sharply. But even to hear his name was sweet and she led Sofia to talk about Rory.

'Please thank the Kyria Julia for the loan,' said Sofia's mother. 'I remember her as a bride, girls. She was so lovely, and we all envied her. But there—it never does, to marry a foreigner. They don't settle, you know. They get homesick for their own country, though by all accounts England is covered with fog all the year round, and it rains every day. Why a man should want to live there—!' She shook her head as if the absurdity of foreigners was too much for her. 'But you're half a foreigner yourself, Evie. Don't you ever want to visit your father's country?'

'Never. This is my country. My mother is Exos-Greek and so am I.'

'Your brother isn't,' the woman said slyly. 'He's an Englishman, or he will be soon. He looks more English every year. And you, Evie, if you take my advice, will put a bit of soft flesh on those bones of yours, or you'll never get a man. They like something to cuddle, don't they, Sofia? I do believe you are thinner than ever these days.'

'And paler,' Sofia added, not quite unkindly. 'You'd look lovely in your new dress if you had more colour. Not that I'd have chosen that strong pattern and dark shade for you, yet it suits you wonderfully. It would look better on me, though. Can I try it on?'

'You're too fat,' Evie rapped. She and Sofia had always shared clothes, but the thought of the other girl in the dress Rory chose did not please her.

Marcus had spent his savings on putting down a deposit for a small café in Nicosia. There was an apartment over it, and Sofia was already putting on the airs of a city-dweller.

'We could have bought a bigger place in Kyrenia or Famagusta,' she told Evie as the two girls sat stitching the trousseau garments under the shade of a pepper tree. 'But Marcus says it is best to be in a fashionable place where the money is. He's ambitious, you see. When we have made a success of a small café, he will move to something larger.'

'More floors to scrub?' Evie said with a smile. 'Oh, I'm so glad for you, Sofia. I'm sure you'll be happy and make lots of money. You do love him, don't you?'

'Naturally I do. But it is also important to have a good living and a home. I am lucky to be getting that, and to like the man too. When we have a bigger place, or maybe if we do well in the small café, you could come and spend the busy season with us if you like. You could earn your keep as a waitress, and we could have a good time together, eh?'

'I'd like that. Would Marcus agree?'

'I'll make him. It was my mother's idea. She said when I'm pregnant next year, I shall need extra help and I must insist on having it. Men give way to a wife when she's having the first baby, so it's a good idea to get into their stupid minds that a women needs help and rest at such times. Afterwards, they take such an idea for granted. But if you let the first time go by without making demands, for ever after they say *Well, you managed the first all right.*'

Evie tried to imagine herself married to Rory, and pricked her finger till the blood made a stain on the seam she was stitching. Her idea of marriage seemed so different from Sofia's. But then Marcus was so different from Rory McDermot.

'Do you think all husbands are the same?' she asked, spitting on the linen and rubbing it with her finger. She bent low over the task so Sofia could not read her face.

'All married women say they are. So they must be. My mother says—'

Marcus arrived, in a new bright blue suit, the day before the wedding. With him came Rory McDermot.

'Would you believe it,' Marcus roared to all and sundry on the quayside, 'we met in Nicosia, and when I told him it was my wedding day today, he said he must come and kiss the bride. Nothing would please him but to come.'

Rory hugged Sofia and handed over the wedding present he had brought, a pair of tall carved candlesticks in olivewood. 'I wish you every happiness, the pair of you. Now, where am I to sleep?'

'Under a tree. Every spare bed in the village is taken up with all the friends and family. Why not walk up to the Villa Julia and ask them to give you a bed there? They did offer, in case we hadn't room down here for everybody who came over from the mainland.'

He shook his head. 'I'd rather not trouble the Kyria Julia. Under a tree will suit me fine.'

In the past weeks he had tramped Cyprus, and slept out more than once. He had walked to the top of the Troodos mountains, seen the beach where the goddess Aphrodite rose newly-created from the foam; he had climbed to the smallest, most remote monastery of them all, perched like a kite upon the summit of Stavrovouni, and knelt in wonder before the silver shrine which held a piece of the True Cross. There he had remembered an argument he had had with his old parish priest as a boy.

'True, my son, there are enough reputed pieces of the True Cross to make a forest, if all were brought together. But sure, if God could make a dinner for five thousand hungry pilgrims out of five little fish and a couple of loaves warm from a good mother's oven, couldn't He make a small forest out of one Cross.' Where's your faith, boy? Do I ask you to believe in a God who is no cleverer than a stupid lad out of an Irish bog, now?'

He had been unhappy. At first, because he had

disappointed a nice girl. But as day followed day, the knowledge grew in him that he loved Evie and not Clodagh. Her lovely oval face haunted his dreams, and the days held no magic because she was not with him.

One man, he had prophesied, you will pierce to the bone and he will love you for ever.

When he remembered those words, he stopped in his tracks and beat his fists upon the green-silver bark of a fig-tree. 'And I am that man!' he cried aloud, startling a goat which had been staring at him with yellow slit eyes. 'I love her. Goat, do you hear me now? I am in love with Evie, in thrall till my life's end. And begod, I could have been her husband this minute if I were not such a fool!'

The solitary walking, the quiet monasteries, the watching ruins full of a millennium's wisdom, convinced him that the first decision was the right one. Not for him, but for the girl herself. How could he let her tie herself down to a wandering man like himself, when she had seen no others? None, of the sort she ought to marry.

He had fought a devil's battle within himself. As day followed day, he wanted her more urgently. The temptation to take a boat for Exos, hurry up the hill and beg her to marry him grew stronger the more he fought it. But the more he loved her, pictured her as he remembered her, half saint and half wild dryad, a creature of trees and water, the more reluctant he felt to hurry her into marriage and responsibilities. Not yet, not yet, he had told himself over and over again. She is not ready; the tree is still in bud. Yet in tortured nights he pictured her hurried into marriage by her mother and uncles, into the hands of a man less able than he to understand her fine delicate quality.

Tired as he was when he flung himself on to whatever bed the night provided, he could not sleep dreamlessly till dawn. But now it was not the running waters of Ireland that sang through his head, the light figure of Clodagh which eluded him like a small lovely ghost slipping through the trees or hurrying before him along the mountain tracks of home.

It was Evie, running lightfooted through the lemon trees. Evie dancing in her blue dress on the quayside, her face pale in moonlight. Evie gravely enquiring about the price of tea at a luxury hotel, or sitting beside him on a green bank above Kyrenia among the scent of rock roses.

Evie saying *I thought perhaps—do you think you could marry me?*

It's this damned climate, he told himself angrily. All these flowers, the scent of lemons, the warmth of the air, the sea shimmering like diamonds, the—the *softness* of everything. It gets under a man's skin. *It is not love!*

It was a long time before he admitted to himself that he was head over heels, deep as the ocean, high as the clouds, in love with Evie. For mile after mile of his solitary, angry walking, he argued with himself, putting forward all the reasons why he couldn't be.

But at last, in the midst of the crowds thronging the Turkish bazaar in Nicosia, he admitted the impossible. Why then, he did not know. Perhaps it was the rolls of gaily coloured cottons for sale, fluttering in the warm wind; or the bright woven baskets, the piles of pink sugared almonds on the stalls.

He bought cheese and fruit for his frugal supper, and his hand shook as he paid for them. Strolling through the covered food market, he fought the desire to make straight for Kyrenia and catch the morning caique for Exos.

Be reasonable, he pleaded with himself. All the arguments for not marrying her remain the same.

Now all the sensible arguments turned against him, and in favour of an immediate departure for the Villa

Julia. What if that mother of hers, with an eye to the cash she coveted, persuaded the girl to marry some rich fat islander coming home to retire? She'd do it, the little fool!

Coming again into the sunlight at the entrance to the covered market, he stopped dead. Something brought Evie to his mind sharply, with a impact like a cutting edge. What was it?

Slowly he turned round, looking for some clue. Was it a girl, or a man from Exos? Someone very like Sofia, perhaps?

Then he laughed, startling a sleepy stallholder. Of course—where else but in the fruit market? It was the scent of lemons.

He took his problem into the high cool mosque at the end of the road. There, barefooted on the rich carpets which were the gifts of the faithful, he sat cross-legged and considered his problem.

So I hurry back and beg her to marry me? She's a girl of spirit, and proud besides, and I hurt her more than somewhat, back there in Kyrenia. Would a lass like that look twice at such a miserable wretch as I, who didn't know enough to catch his luck on the wing when it went by? If she spoke to me at all, which is unlikely, she'd give me the sharp point of her tongue which is all I'd deserve.

But suppose—just suppose for one moment—that she forgave you, boyo, and married you? How then? Wouldn't it mean the loss of the fine dream you've been dreaming? The final severance of the thread that binds you to Clodagh and all she stands for? To marry Evie would mean settling for good on the island of Exos, living in the Villa Julia and—

He slapped one hand into the other. Rory McDermot, he said aloud in the vast silence of the mosque, you are worse than a fool. Isn't that what started the whole thing? That you wanted to do just that—settle on Exos and live in the Villa Julia?

Not with a wife, he protested faintly. I hadn't included wife and children in the picture; nor a mother-in-law. Nor becoming second cousin by marriage to the whole population!

He collected his pack, slung it over his shoulder and marched purposefully back to the Greek side of the barrier. If there was enough money in his account at the bank—and there should be, if that American magazine had paid promptly for the three pieces they had bought—he planned to book a flight to the States. He had always had a fancy to take a look at Arizona.

The money was not there. No matter, he knew how to wait, and there was much to see in Nicosia. The temple of the dancing dervishes, now. That sounded interesting. Tomorrow—

Three days later, coming out of the bank with money in his pocket, he met Marcus.

The Greek seized his hand, planted a garlicky kiss on each of his cheeks, and hurried him off to look at the café he had bought.

'You must come to the wedding, *kyrios*. Sofia will be angry with me if I do not take you.'

'Sofia will tear my ears off! I'd never get away alive!'

'Nonsense, nonsense! She's a sensible girl. She never really believed you had all that money, and once I'd started to buy the café—' he shrugged and kissed his bunched fingers, 'she was mine.'

'Always was, Marcus. And—Evie?'

'Too thin, don't you think? Thinner than ever. That girl is unhappy, Rory. I think she'll leave Exos pretty soon.'

Rory's heart turned over painfully. Why was he wasting time here, talking idly, when Evie might be leaving the island tomorrow and he would never find her?

Marcus went on, 'I mean, she's not content where she is. She's half a northerner, you know. Always on the move, they are. Always wanting to get something done, if it's only moving from here to there as fast as world go by. Same as yourself, sir. Now you're a man their legs can carry them. Can't rest and watch the on the go.'

'My dear Marcus, you slander me! I want nothing more than to take root on a cliff overlooking the sea, and vegetate. All right, I'll be glad to come to the wedding if you'll have me.'

And so on the night before Sofia's wedding, he left the bridegroom's rowdy party early and took his sleeping bag up on to the headland, from whence he could look down on the lights of the Villa Julia.

She is sleeping down there, he told himself; and then grinned at finding himself out in such a youthful sentiment. Be your age, boyo, he said aloud, and immediately fell to picturing Evie asleep, soft-mouthed and relaxed, her hand under her cheek, the long straight yellow hair spread like a net over the pillow.

When the last light went out in the villa, he inserted himself into the narrow sleeping bag and lay awake planning his campaign. He would not go straight to her and expect to begin where they left off. That would be boorish, and taking advantage of the fact that she had proposed to him in a desperate effort to save her home.

It mustn't be like that. If she came to him, it must be in love and because she wanted him and no other. If he could win her that way, well and good. But there must be no question of her saying yes merely to keep the villa in the family. Softly now, old Rory my lad. She's high-spirited and timid both. This will need patience, and guile besides.

Evie was not asleep. She lay awake thinking about Sofia, wondering how a girl felt on her wedding eve, and what she thought about. Wondering if such a night would ever come to her now. Her body, like a traitor, longed for Rory, remembering with sharp sweetness his kiss, his touch, his voice. She knew with every nerve that if his hand touched her out of ten thousand, she would recognise his touch. Her skin remembered him. There were times when tears forced themselves from under her closed eyelids because of the emptiness he had left in her heart.

But in spite of the moonlight flooding the room, the soft murmurs of the night, the feel of happiness in the air because of tomorrow's wedding, Evie turned away from thoughts of Rory with bitter memories, of their last minutes together. Remembering his gentle refusal of her proposal of marriage, she burned with anguished embarrassment. Why, oh, why had she done such a stupid thing? Now he would never, never come back to Exos.

The village was astir before sunrise. There was much to be done before the dew was off the ground. The outdoor ovens were swept out, and fresh wood piled inside them to smoulder redly until the metal lining was hot enough to cook the whole lambs and kids for the evening's feast. When the wood was consumed to ash, the men would sweep it out; pack in the joints, fit the heavy iron doors and seal them with a small boulder. Meantime there was the charcoal fire to light under the water-driven communal spit, the long metal spears to be loaded with chickens and lobsters to be cooked later in the charcoal's heat. It was a delicate art, understood best—so they insisted—by the old men of the village, to judge the exact distance between fire and meat, the precise drip of water from the aged brass taps which would turn the many spits at the right speed. Not too fast or the meat wouldn't brown; not too slow, or it would burn.

Sofia lay in bed listening to the chatter and bustle. A fierce argument blew up beneath her window and died away. She sighed contentedly. This was her day. She was the bride. Tomorrow and all the tomorrows she would have to get up as early as the others; earlier, when she was working with Marcus in their café. But today she could stretch luxuriously, smile at herself in her looking glass, and think about her wedding dress, the short white veil, the little bridal crown set with pearls.

She had no illusions about marriage. Being a wife didn't make life easier or more rosy for a woman, but at least one was one's own mistress and under no one's thumb but one's husband's. And, playing the cards right, that wasn't too bad. A clever woman, well schooled by a clever mother, could manage a man without his knowing it. She smiled to herself, stretched and yawned. As long as youth and beauty lasted, she could manage Marcus. After that—she grimaced and shrugged— after that, she would be *Mama,* with a family firmly under her thumb.

Julia and Evie were already busy in their kitchen, baking little biscuits sweet with grapefruit-blossom honey. They had had a brisk difference of opinion over what they should wear, but that was settled now. Evie would wear her new sea-blue dress, made by Julia in the style sketched by Rory. Julia would wear the old traditional dress she had lent her daughter for the dance on the quay. That her waist was still slim enough was a matter of pride with her, and for once she meant to show off among her friends. Not one of them, Julia was convinced, could still wear the dress she had been married in.

'It should be you,' Julia grumbled. 'We shall have to find a husband for you, Evie, though how, I don't know. Luckily you have your dowry, which should get you a good man. Where am I to look, in God's name? When your father answers the advertisement—'

Evie said patiently, 'Mama, he won't. It's too long ago, nearly three months. I shouldn't have told you what I'd done. I'm sorry I even agreed to the lawyer putting advertisements in. It has only roused hopes in you, my poor lamb. Darling, we must really make ourselves believe he's dead.'

'That I will never do, till I have proof. He will come, or send. Then I shall be able to do something about a marriage for you. Why should Sofia be a bride and not you? Do you want me shamed before all my friends and family, eh?'

Evie felt choked with exasperation. There were times when she felt like shaking her mother hard, to knock the obstinacy out of her. Why couldn't she listen to common sense? After all these years, it was absurd to suppose a man would arrive home one day in time for supper as if nothing had happened.

'Finish the biscuits,' she said crossly. 'I have to go outside a minute.' Another second in the kitchen, listening to that eternally hopeful story about George Marsden's return, would be the very last straw.

She found Georgi patiently trotting back and forth from the thin trickle of the stream to the vegetable garden, watering the precious plants before the sun got too high. All the island was arid now, the bare earth showing tan and yellow.

'They've begun!' the boy shouted, pointing down to

the village like a white toy below. 'Look at the smoke! They'll be making the most enormous kebabs on the spit. How soon can I go down?'

'Finish the work first,' she said automatically, and was appalled to hear her voice sounding exactly like her mother's. I *am* growing like her, she thought in a panic. I do nothing but work, and think about nothing but Rory coming back, even though I know in my bones he never will. In no time at all, I'll be old.

She snatched the yellow plastic bucket from her young brother. 'Put on your wedding suit and go now. I'll finish your jobs. Hurry or you'll miss some of the fun.' She laughed and hugged him tightly. 'Oh, I'm sorry, Georgi. I don't play with you any more, eh? But I will, I promise. Being unhappy is silly when you can't do anything to change things. Run along. We're all going to have a wonderful day.'

The boy raced into the house to change. Evie took the bucket to the stream. From today on, she would stop thinking about the past and look forward into a future which did not include Rory McDermot. She had longed to believe that he would follow her to Exos. The fact that he had not done so was proof that he did not, could not, love her, and even the bait of possessing the Villa Julia was not enough to persuade him to marry her.

Detestable man! She crouched down beside the stream, noticing with concern that the water would not last much longer. I ought to hate him. Perhaps I do? They say love turns to hate, and when a man is so stupid as to go on loving a woman who wouldn't have him—well, why shouldn't I hate him!

Temper rose and choked her. She threw the yellow bucket away from her violently, so it bounced on the glinting stones. Damn him, damn him, I'd like to hit him! She clenched her fists and beat them on her knees, letting wave after wave of bottled-up rage sweep through her, exhausting her anger till at last she bent over the limpid water and buried her face in her hands. She had not cried before, but the hurt and frustration of the last months eased themselves now in a wild torrent of tears and shuddering.

Quiet at last, she splashed cold water over her face, then went to catch and saddle her mother's donkey before changing to go down to the wedding.

They went straight to the bride's house, disregarding the excitement on the quay where the caique from Kyrenia was disembarking a crowd of guests in their best clothes and laden with gifts.

Sofia was dressed except for the crown, which her mother was now pinning on her hair. 'Here's Kyria Julia,' someone cried. 'Let her do it. After all, it's hers. She should know the proper way to fix it.'

Sofia grinned at Evie and mouthed, *'You next!'* as the two mothers fussed gently over the arranging of the crown and veil. There was no time for talk between the girls, but Sofia gave Evie a quick hug and whispered, 'It's your lucky day. I'm the bride and I know who's lucky and who isn't. Something wonderful is going to happen for you today, Evie.'

'That's good. You wouldn't care to say what? I bet you don't know. You've said the same to every single girl on the island already.'

Sofia's grin became more tormenting than before. 'Oh no, I haven't. There's a surprise for you. Wait and see.'

Evie shivered with expectancy, and her palms grew damp. 'You mean, you really know something? Is—is anybody coming with the caique?' She could not make her lips form Rory's name.

Sofia shook her head, but carefully because of the crown. 'No, nothing like that. But I have at least twenty male cousins expected, and that probably means forty will arrive. Surely that's enough to choose from, even for a faddy creature like you?'

The hope died. All Sofia meant was that out of all her relatives at the wedding, her friend might make a match with one. But Sofia couldn't possibly know that if Evie Marsden didn't marry Rory McDermot, who wasn't coming, she would never marry anyone.

'Sofia, stop teasing. You've got love on the brain, and why shouldn't you, on your wedding morning? Listen, isn't that the bridegroom's party arriving? It's time to go. Oh, Sofia, be very happy!'

Sudden tears brimmed the bride's eyes. 'Evie! I don't want it all to happen. I'll be so lonely in Nicosia, away from everybody.'

Evie carefully wiped the trembling tears so they did not fall. 'You're *not to cry*! If you do, you'll look terrible. You'll have Marcus all to yourself, and your own home, and you'll be able to see the shops and all the rich tourists. Smile! That's better. Off you go!'

It was after the solemn part of the morning, when the bride's and bridegroom's friends and family began to mingle, that Evie came face to face with Rory.

She lifted her eyes to the tall figure who stood in her path, and there he was. Her heart beat painfully, and she felt the colour drain from her face.

'Rory!' she whispered. 'What are you ... what are you doing here?'

'The same as you. Attending a friend's wedding. Surprised to see me?'

She saw that he was thinner and browner. He wore a new and more shapely suit and a good shirt, which surprised her, for somehow she had never pictured him in anything but the shabby jacket and faded shirts in which she had seen him so often.

133

'You look very smart,' she said stupidly. So often, she had dreamed of this first meeting, but in dreams there are no words to be said.

He smiled. 'So do you. The dress, I take it, is the result of our shopping?'

'Yes. But I am still wearing the red shoes which you disliked so much.' She forced herself to remain calm, to keep her voice cool and controlled.

'I'm afraid you found me abominably rude about them.'

'It doesn't matter. All that is a long time ago. I've forgotten what you actually said, and it wasn't of the slightest importance.'

'Some of it was,' he said deeply. 'I've been kicking myself ever since for not jumping on that caique and coming back with you that day.'

She shrugged. 'There has been a caique in from Kyrenia every day except Sunday. If you had wanted to come, there was nothing to stop you.'

Her coldness frightened him. There was not a spark of expression in her icy voice, no light in the eyes which looked at him as if he did not really exist. His heart sank. He had a long way to go, and it might be too late even to begin.

'I didn't come before,' he said carefully, 'because I wanted to be sure there was nothing left over from the past. I wanted the years ahead to be free of . . . of memories. I wanted to get things straight in my mind.'

She clasped her hands so he should not see them trembling. 'And now you are satisfied with your own state of mind?'

'Far from it. But I should be a good deal happier than I have been, if I thought we could start our friendship all over again on a better footing.'

'It's three months,' she told him flatly. 'There are

other things in my life now. I don't think our friendship, even on a new footing, could have any real future.'

The sight of him had robbed her of coherent thought. All she remembered was her anger of two hours ago, the long sobbing by the brook, the lost sleep; the fury of frustration which had swept her from time to time in the last three months. She would not go through all that again. If she had to live her life without him, she could not begin too soon the painful process of erasing him from her heart.

'Can't we even try, Evie?' His voice was harsh. He had not expected so much enmity. She had changed. Where was the warmth, the spontaneity which to him was Evie? Now he looked at her more closely, he saw that she was paler, her eyes were dark smudged, the delicate bone structure in her face thrown into relief by her thinness. 'We were doing so well, that afternoon up by the monastery, when we visited St. Polystemon.'

She turned away slightly. 'That afternoon contains much that I prefer to forget, *kyrie*. You must understand . . . I was driven to desperation by the need to save the villa and the land for my brother. There was nothing more to it than that. I hope you didn't read anything . . . anything into my foolishness that I didn't mean?'

'I understood that. I have never flattered myself that I . . . meant anything to you, in a personal way. Only that you needed to keep the house in the family. That's why . . . I mean, I could hardly let you sacrifice yourself. I can take it you have now made other and more satisfactory arrangements?' There was a faint tinge of bitter humour in his voice. He had never allowed himself to think, for a moment, that she felt any more than friendliness towards him, but he had left himself room for hope. It hurt more than somewhat to have it spelled out so clearly in that icy little tone.

'I have seen a lawyer about our affairs. I hope to hear something from England very soon.'

'I see. Then may I wish you every success in your endeavours?'

The crowd which had swept them together now swept them apart, as a stentorian voice invited them all to sit down and eat. The main meal, still cooking in the adobe ovens, would be served after dark, but now there was fish, hot and succulent, baked in vine leaves, and enough sweet red wine to float a fishing boat. Evie had promised to help serve the guests and hurried away to her duties.

So Rory was Sofia's 'surprise'? He must have arrived on the island last night, since he had not come with the morning's boat. If he had loved her, he would surely have come up at once to the villa to find her. That he had not done so seemed proof that she meant little to him. Only a casual friend, to be set down or picked up as the mood took him.

The meeting had been disastrous, but at least one good had come out of it. She had been able to make him understand quite clearly that her proposal of marriage had been entirely a matter of business and that his help was not now needed. After what she had said today, he would never even suspect that she loved him.

The day wore on. After midday, when the heat was intense and the trees cast no shade, the older folk withdrew to sleep off the wine and strong coffee laced with brandy, in which they had been indulging for hours. The girls, among them Evie, washed the glasses and re-laid the tables ready for the real business of eating and drinking later. The children went swimming, so many excited small brown frogs in the clear water. The bride and bridegroom disappeared.

So the waterfront was deserted when a neat white launch put in from Kyrenia, carrying two passengers.

Only Rory, half asleep on a tilted chair under a date palm, saw them land.

Tourists, he thought, noting the camera, the smart cream blazer of the man, the white dress and lobster-red arms of the woman. Too bad! Nobody free to take them a trip round the island; nobody even awake at the *taverna* to produce the tea an English lady would be demanding in—he glanced at his watch—about half an hour from now.

He watched them, from under the brim of his hat, not because he cared what they did, but because there was nothing else to watch. They walked the length of the waterfront and back, talking seriously and looking at the houses more closely than the normal run of tourists.

Bemused as he was with too much food and drink, it took Rory some time to reach the conclusion that they were looking for someone, or something. He brought the front legs of his chair to the ground with a thump. By St. Patrick, what a dolt he was! They had probably come to the wedding and were bewildered to find not a living soul about.

He strolled towards them and raised his battered straw. 'Can I help you? Everybody else is asleep, I believe. Have you come to the wedding?'

The woman's face lit up. A pleasant, thirtyish kind of face, interested in everything. Not the man's wife. His elder sister, maybe. 'Is there a wedding? Oh, how lovely! I do hope we can see some of it. We rather hoped to stay on the island overnight. Is there a hotel?'

'Not one I'd recommend for you, ma'am. Only the *taverna*, and every bed in that is occupied three deep. Myself, I slept under a tree last night, but there are apt to be snakes. It might do for the gentleman, but not for you.'

She glanced at her companion, dismayed. 'Oh, Peter,

what a shame! We shall have to go back to Kyrenia tonight.'

The man grinned and nodded towards the *taverna*. 'I'd prefer it, if that's the only hotel. The fact is,' he turned to Rory, 'you may be able to help us. We're here on business, and I'm not sure how many people here speak English.'

'All of them. Same like Cyprus. Some better and some worse, but anyone you'd be likely to do business with will be all right. Only with the wedding and all, it's not a business day. You and your boatmen will be welcome to stay for supper, that I do know. But not to talk shop. Everyone will be too busy eating, drinking, singing and dancing to bother. If you stay, you'll see something out of the ordinary tourist run, and I assure you you'll be made welcome. Everybody is, and there's enough food for two regiments of Foot and a Brigade of Guards besides.'

The woman pleaded, 'Do let's, Peter. We've got the launch for the whole day and the boatmen won't mind if it's a wedding. Go and ask them, there's a dear. After all, it is a holiday first and foremost. The business is only incidental. We can do that by letter if we have to.'

The boy smiled. Fresh, young, good-looking, English. Comfortably off, Rory noted. 'All right, Anna. Half a tick, I'll talk to them. Oh, by the way, sir, my name's Peter Brown. My sister, Anna Brown.'

Rory clicked heels, bowed, and introduced himself. 'I could probably rustle up a pot of tea if you'd care to sit under the palms a while, Miss Brown. It may take time. Will you take lemon with it? Unless you really like goat's milk, of course. Some people do.'

Anna shuddered and said she would take lemon.

As there was no one in the kitchen of the *taverna* and heavy snoring came from the room above, Rory made the tea himself, and carried it out on a tray. 'I've brought three glasses, in the hope that I may join you.'

'Please do,' said Peter cheerfully. 'You've been most awfully kind. My sister was dying for a cuppa. So was I, as a matter of fact. Oh, and lemon. Good. You're Irish, aren't you? Do you live here?'

'Not exactly.'

Anna indicated the tea tray with a gesture. 'But a privileged visitor, I'm sure. Do you know many people on Exos? My brother and I are looking for an English family, a widow and two children. I wonder if you've met a Mrs. George Marsden here?'

Rory opened his mouth to deny any knowledge of an English widow before he recognised Evie's mother under the description. 'I've met her,' he admitted cautiously.

A shiver of fear crisped his nerves, like a breath of icy wind ruffling the warm calm sea. This well-dressed pair, so English, so entirely foreign to the palm-edged island, seemed to him to threaten the untroubled existence of his delicate, silvery Evie. He felt them as the outriders of the materialistic ugly age he hated. As they sipped the hot tea from tiny tulip-shaped glasses, he heard with his mind's ears the roaring technology of which the island hardly dreamed. Here was danger for Evie, from which all his love might not be able to protect her.

'Kyria Julia Marsden is not English,' he told them. 'She is Exos-Greek. Her son and daughter probably resemble their father, both being fair. The boy has blue eyes, but Evie's are—' he paused, remembering Evie's serious eyes resting on him with a questioning look. 'Grey, I think; except when they are blue. They change, like water under the sky. Are you by any chance related?'

The woman answered. 'Our family firm act as Mr.

George Marsden's lawyers. My brother and I were due for a holiday anyway, and when we discovered his widow lived here, we decided to fly out and visit her, rather than write. I've always wanted to see Cyprus, and the advertisement gave us a splendid excuse.'

'Advertisement?'

'A clerk in the office always watches the agony column in the national dailies, Mr.—er—'

'McDermot. You mean someone advertised for news of George?'

'Exactly. Of course *we* advertised at the time he was drowned, six years ago. But no one replied at the time, so we were pleased when—'

She went on explaining, but Rory was not listening. His world, his new golden world, in which he loved and won Evie, and lived with her in a white house on the edge of a sea-cliff, had shattered into a thousand pieces.

Lawyers don't fly across Europe to visit the widow of a poor man, holiday or no. These two had come on business and their business was concerned with wills and estates. George Marsden was dead; and there was cash in the kitty. Maybe a good deal of it.

What could a poor devil of an impecunious Irishman do now but shoulder his bag and away? Having refused the girl when she had no more fortune than he, how could he now turn up on her doorstep as an eager suitor?

He cut through Anna's talk. 'If I'm right, that advertisement must have been inserted months ago, when Evie went to Kyrenia. What kept you?'

'Legal affairs move slowly. It wasn't that we neglected the Marsden business, only that our office is like most, chronically overworked and understaffed. We needed to gather a fair amount of information, from the Kyrenia lawyer and from our own records. All the material is six years old, remember.'

Rory rubbed his ear. 'I wasn't complaining, only thinking it would have been a sight more convenient to me, if you'd stayed away a few days longer. There's nobody at home at the Villa Julia today, but if you sit here you'll meet the whole family before long. Anyone will point them out. Me, I'm leaving. There'll be no man sober enough to take a fishing boat out tonight, but maybe I might beg a lift of you, when you're ready to leave?'

CHAPTER SEVEN

AS he turned the corner of the *taverna*, intending to fetch his bag, he ran into Evie and a stout perspiring youth in an elegant suit too tight for him.

'Hello,' Evie greeted Rory with a detectable note of relief in her voice. 'This is Theo. He's teaching me Italian. We're going to hang up extra lanterns on the waterfront.'

'You're not,' Rory told her firmly. He took her share of the lanterns and piled them into Theo's arms with a dazzling smile. '*Arrivederci,* Theo my boy. I must have a long serious talk with Miss Marsden.'

'Poor Theo!' Evie sighed. 'He meant well, but his admiration was a bit hard to bear. I want a long serious talk with you too, Mr. McDermot, to say I'm sorry I was so bad-tempered about the red shoes. You were right, of course. Why can't we ever meet without quarrelling? It's mostly me. I'll never be a plaster saint, will I?'

'You won't, God be thanked. Do you think I'd like you as much if you were? Now listen, this is important. I've news for you.'

'What sort of news? What's Georgi been up to?' Her eyes widened with fear. 'You said serious? He's not in trouble, is he? Or Mama?'

'I haven't seen either of them since the ceremony. This concerns you. Let's go in the church. It's the only cool place where we can be sure of being alone for a while.'

Sobered by his tone, she let him lead her into the tiny dark church; empty now, and quiet. 'What is it, Rory?

'As soon as a boat leaves the island, I must be on my way. This must be our own private goodbye. I . . . I have business elsewhere.'

'No,' she said in a choking whisper. 'Please, no. Rory, I can't bear it if you go away again. All this summer I . . .' Pressing her lips tightly together, she twisted her head away from him. He felt her trembling.

Now was the moment he could have taken her in his arms, found her mouth with his, kissed her into warm awareness of love. If only that darned lawyer had kept away till tomorrow! His arms went out towards her, and only a searing effort of will held him back. What sort of man coaxed a woman to love him five minutes after he'd heard she had money coming to her? And before she herself knew?

His grandda, that wise old fool, had warned him once that there was a lot of marriage spent out of bed, and a lot of years to face. And if the day ever came when Evie was his wife, he wanted to face those years with his self-respect intact. She must never be able to throw at him the accusation that she had not had a chance to see the world and spend her money, get what she wanted or thought she wanted from the great oyster now opening before her.

Nor—come to that—did he ever want to know himself a rich woman's lap dog, and end by being despised by her and everybody else.

'There will be more summers, and other interests in your life, Evie my dear. The world is a wonderful place, and when you've seen it, you may come home and choose this one spot for your own. Or again, you may not.'

'I've noticed nobody seems to like this famous world of yours very much. Everybody who comes here comes to get away from it. All I want is Exos . . . and the . . . people . . . I love.'

143

He sighed and stroked her hair, feeling the silk of it under his hand. 'You are so young, mavourneen. And so lovely. And so damned ignorant. Promise me you won't marry any man till you've had an opportunity of meeting more than the islanders and a stray tourist or two?'

'I promise you I won't marry any man till I can marry the man I truly love. Why are we talking like this? And why are you going away so soon? You won't get a boat off the island tonight and tomorrow everybody will be sleeping off the effects.'

She was quivering with his nearness, and hard put to it to prevent herself flinging her arms round him and begging him not to go. She could keep the promise she had made, very easily. She would marry no one but Rory. Why didn't he understand that? She had told him she loved him, as strongly as she dared. Did he want it spelling out? Oh, if he had loved her just the smallest bit, he would have understood what she meant.

She could say no more. For the moment she was unable to speak and had no intention of letting herself be hurt more than he had hurt her already. Not to be twice rejected.

Close together, in silence, they stood a long minute in the dim church. The gold gleamed on the icons. The pale painted face of St. Polystemon hung like a narrow moon in the dusk.

Evie felt crushed, lost, forlorn. The secret hope of Rory's return had buoyed her up over the worst moments of his absence. Now the break would be final. He had come back, and was going away again. The lovely moment when he had stroked her hair so tenderly was no more than a compassion, such as he might have felt for a lost kitten.

'Come along now.' He broke the hush at last.

'Time for your news. And it is not I who must tell it.'

At the door he held her in front of him, touching her bare arms, feeling the warmth of her body close to his. The scent of her hair was in his nostrils.

'There's a new boat in the harbour,' she marvelled. 'Someone late for the wedding?'

'Someone to see *you*. And that's the boat I'll be going out in, when it leaves. Look under the palm trees, at the end table. Do you see that charming young man in the fine suit, and his sister with him?'

'Tourists? She's thin like me, and that's an elegant dress she's wearing. Looks expensive.'

'So do her handbag, shoes, and plain gold jewellery. You like it?'

She shivered, suddenly afraid. 'Who are they? Why am I to look at them?'

'Dear girl, you've guessed for some time that your father is dead?'

She had known it in her heart, yet the certainty touched her like an icy hand. She moistened dry lips. 'Yes, I guessed.'

'Those two are lawyers. They will tell your mother there is money to come from his estate—probably enough for all her needs and yours. Enough for Georgi.'

She covered her face with her hands. 'I don't want it. Our lives will be changed. Money will hurt us. I can see it as evil. Please, Rory, tell me how to send them away.'

His grip firmed on her quivering shoulders. 'You can't do that. Your mother must be told. This is your future. Stick your chin up and go out to meet it.'

'Alone?'

'Not for long. Those two are kind, and friendly; they've taken the trouble to come all the way from

145

England to talk to you in person. That's better than a formal letter. On your way.' He gave her a gentle push.

'I feel sick. Am I tidy?'

He studied her gravely. 'Wait a minute.' Taking a comb from his pocket, he straightened her hair. 'That's better.' He stooped and kissed her lightly on the lips. 'It's been grand knowing you, Princess. Now it's goodbye to the beggarman and hop up with you on to your throne.'

'Rory—please. Come with me.'

'Away with you,' he said.

Rory waited, watching the slight figure cover the distance between the church door and the table under the palms. Straight and tall she walked, her head high. Walking into her future like a queen, he thought, and God go with her.

Some day, one day, she may come back. She may look at the world and find it wanting, and come back home looking for the beggarman who loves her. I'll be there, Princess, when and if you want me, he vowed silently.

Then he cursed himself for a sentimental Irishman who believed in fairies, swung on his heel and marched away up to the far end of the harbour, to wait quiet till the boat went. Ach, you're going soft, boyo, he told himself. Did you ever hear such a load of old codswallop as you've been dreaming this last twenty-four hours? Be off with you; find somewhere the wind blows cold and hard, and great waves smash on great rocks all day and all night. Get stuck into some real work for a change.

'*Kalimera!* My name is Evie Marsden. You were looking for me?'

Her arrival brought Peter Brown to his feet. He stood six feet tall, was as slim as a willow, and his fair hair was bleached by the sun. A golden youth, like the gods of mythology; a young Apollo. In her delight at something so unexpected and so perfect, Evie forgot her fears and smiled at him, a smile of pure pleasure.

Anna introduced them both and asked her to sit down. 'It must have been you who had the advertisement put in? We're grateful to you, Miss Marsden. You see, if your father's estate—money, that is—was not claimed in fifteen years, it might have been forfeited to the Government. And I do hate paying money to governments unnecessarily.'

'When did he die?'

'Six years ago,' Peter answered the question. 'He sold a house and some land left to him by an aunt, and bought a good yacht. We were told he intended sailing her out to the Mediterranean, so presumably he was coming home.'

'Tell my mother that. She'll be glad to know. What happened then?'

'A sudden squall in the Channel. The lifeboats had a number of calls that night, up and down the south coast. Mr. Marsden's yacht and another were in collision and both were lost. The other sailor was rescued, with his wife and son. Your father was probably knocked unconscious by the mast, and his body swept away.'

'And never found?'

'Oh yes,' Anna said gently, 'they found him. He was buried at Plymouth. The aunt must have been his only surviving relative, for we discovered no one else at all, although we advertised as we always do in such cases. There was insurance on his life, and on the boat.'

'Why did he stay away so long?'

'Men get homesick. Who knows, maybe he wanted to

establish himself in England again, and send for you all, or fetch you? Selling the house suggests he'd given up that idea, if idea it was. That must be his secret now. We don't know why he left here in the first place. A wife and children, and such a beautiful place to live? It seems unbelievable. Yet one can't be a lawyer long without finding out that men do some unaccountable things for ridiculously small reasons.'

'One needn't be a lawyer to find that out, Miss Brown. I know it. May I ask a favour, please?'

Peter said heartily, 'Ask away.' His eyes had never left Evie, and she was uncomfortably aware of his eager gaze. It was not unlike Theo's.

'Need you tell my mother till tomorrow? It is a wedding today, and a bereavement would spoil everything. Out of respect for the dead—'

'But George Marsden hasn't been on the island for almost ten years, isn't that so?'

'My mother is bereaved, and my brother and I fatherless. Do you think no one will care or notice, Mr. Brown?'

'I'm sorry. It seemed such a long time ago. People have long memories here, it seems.'

'Do they forget so quickly, where you live? Don't they care for the griefs of their neighbours? I don't think I care much for your England.'

'You must see it,' Anna put in quickly, covering her brother's confusion. 'It's your father's country, and he would have liked you to know something of it. Your brother too. He's an Englishman, after all. Why don't you pay us a visit and see London? My mother loves visitors and was so interested in the reason for our coming here. Oh—Peter! I've just remembered, we can't stay overnight, there's nowhere to sleep. I'm afraid we'll have to hire the boat another day. Will it be too expensive?'

148

'Come in the caique,' Evie suggested. 'That's not nearly so expensive as hiring a launch all to yourself. But why must you go back? We have rooms empty at the Villa Julia, and it would be inhospitable not to offer you beds. My mother won't question it. With so many visitors on the island, she'd be surprised if we didn't have the house full.'

Brother and sister exchanged glances. 'I'd love to,' said Anna, 'if that is no trouble.'

Peter reminded her that they had promised the Irishman a lift back to Cyprus.

'Tomorrow will do for him,' Evie told them firmly. 'Anyway, if your boatmen come to the wedding feast— and they will—they won't be taking a boat to sea this night. Excuse me, I'll go and arrange it with Mama now. And you will keep your promise? Not a word till tomorrow?'

Peter lifted her hand and touched it with his lips. 'We promise, both of us. One more night can't hurt. If there's dancing, will you dance with me?'

'Peter—' his sister warned, 'perhaps Miss Marsden does not want to dance. She knows, if her mother doesn't.'

'To be honest, Miss Brown, I hardly remember Father. Tonight I shall remember I have come into a fortune, eh? And think about the things I can buy with my money. There will be dancing and I shall dance. Tomorrow will be the time for mourning.'

'Very sensible, my dear. Won't you call me Anna? and say Peter? This is not a lawyer's office, we're on holiday and tired of formality. What will you buy?'

'If you'll say Evie, I will tell you. I shall buy St. Polystemon's skull. It's time he came back home, poor boy. I shall buy—no, wait. I have to think. I must go now. Have a look round the village. The church is good, so our visitors tell us. You'll have some luggage in the boat? I'll send someone to carry it up. Theo will do it, and Georgi will help. Georgi is my brother and as soon as I can find him—'

She hurried away, knowing exactly what she must do.

'That girl's excited,' Anna remarked as she strolled with Peter towards the whitewashed church. 'Did you see the realisation of money hit her suddenly, almost in mid-sentence? Funny how it does that to people. I hope it won't go to her head.'

'She's a knock-out, Anna, an absolute knock-out. Can you imagine what she'll be like in good clothes and with that hair properly done? Got her beautiful head screwed on the right way too. She saw at once that if the news broke tonight, it would dish the party. We mustn't let her waste her cash on buying up old Thingummyjig's head, though. Wasn't that the one we saw yesterday, at the monastery? Cures barrenness in women?'

'That was St. Somebody's belt, love. Don't you go turning the child's head. She's young, beautiful, rich, and a novelty. But novelties don't always transplant. She may be a bit of a freak in London. She had bare feet.'

'And gorgeous legs,' Peter reminded her dreamily. 'Mother will enjoy dressing her. I say, I've just had a dreadful thought. The mama may want to come too. Well, that'll be your responsibility. You invited them.'

'We owe it to them. Part of this holiday goes on a perfectly legitimate expense account, remember. Don't be so solemn, little brother. Ten days in London doing the sights and they'll be on the plane to Nicosia laden with new clothes and presents for all the island cousins-once-removed, and we shall neatly remove George Marsden from our files for ever.'

'Famous last words! I may want to marry that girl.'

'Idiot!' said his sister fondly as they entered the church, blinking.

Evie found Theo fixing lanterns, scooped Georgi out of the water, and explained what had to be done. Georgi sulked, but the chance of going aboard the smart launch was too good to be missed, so he pulled his shirt over his head and trotted off beside Theo.

Now, before the people started drifting back to the centre of things, she had to find Rory and tell him the rest of the story about her father. She stood still, concentrating; trying to read herself into his mind. He had said goodbye to her, so he did not mean to see her again. If he came to the party he would stay with the men. At this moment, those men who were awake would be clustered around the communal spit watching the long kebab spears turning; or bringing up the wine from cool cellars.

Not there.

Already the tables were filling up. Laughing, chattering, teasing, giggling, in their different ways the people of Exos gathered for the wedding feast. It was too late. Rory would drift back with the men, take a seat among them, apart from the women as was the custom. Unless and until a man left his chair and joined the crowd, no woman could approach him. Such a thing simply was not done. So bold a creature would lower herself, make her man a laughing stock, a henpecked weakling. And Rory knew it.

There were other unwritten laws to be obeyed. The law of hospitality, for instance. The Browns must be presented to the bride and groom, and to their hostess.

Anna had provided herself with a wedding present, a carved wooden donkey with panniers, bought that morning in Kyrenia.

'That was for Mother,' Peter protested. His sister told

him to shut up and search his overnight bag for a gift for the groom. Shaving lotion or something.

Julia was graciousness itself. 'I wonder if you happen to know my husband?' Evie heard her saying. 'I'm expecting him home any time, but just now I believe he is in England.'

Evie grabbed Peter. 'Dance with me. I'll send someone to rescue your sister. Hi, Andreas . . . the English lady needs a partner.'

Andreas scratched his good-natured head. 'But will she mind dancing with me? She doesn't know me.'

'Dance!' shouted Evie imperiously as the music swept her by in an ever-growing circle. When she saw Anna safely dancing, she changed places with Sofia, who was not so much married that she could not appreciate the novelty of partnering a good-looking foreigner and pushing him through the movements of the dance.

Evie stole away. She knew, now, where Rory would be.

She saw nobody as she walked through the lemon grove, which was sheltered by high hedges of thick elephant grass. Nobody under the fig tree, nobody on the path past the Villa Julia and up to the headland. Everybody for miles around was dancing or drinking, working up an appetite for the feast. Even here, high up on the mountain, the faint smell of lamb baked with herbs made itself felt.

Out at last on to the headland, where the wind off the sea blew her thin dress close to her body. Balancing along the flat stone and marble slabs which had once been a temple floor.

He was there, in the ruined temple, sitting with his back to one of her headless statues. His hands were clasped round his knees. He was staring up at the darkening sky, at the first star of the evening. There was a glint of tears on his face.

'Rory!' She spoke softly, but he heard. He leapt to his feet as he saw her coming, and opened his arms to receive her.

'Oh, Rory, Rory! I've been such a fool! Why didn't I tell you months ago that I love you? Do you hear, my darling? I love you.'

She saw the wild joy on his face. Then his mouth sought hers. They were pressed close, body to body, oblivious of everything but the warmth and young firmness of flesh and bone, of racing blood and quivering nerves. As they kissed hungrily again and again, he rocked her in his arms.

At last he said, 'I'd no idea it was like this with you, beloved. I've loved you for months. I fought it, for your sake. I ought to be fighting it now, but you caught me in a weak moment ...'

'You were crying.'

'That's the hell of it. I was. I'd lost you through my own stupid fault. I let the image of Clodagh come between us, not understanding that it was only an image, a memory in the mirror. When you ... when you asked me to marry you, all those weeks ago, did you love me then?'

'Of course. Would I want to marry a man I didn't love?'

'But you said ...'

She covered his mouth with her hand. 'To save my pride, Rory. Only to save my pride. But when pride is beaten down, love gets a chance. Earlier today, even, I wouldn't say the words which were fighting to get out. But when at last I understood that you were going away again, and this time it would be for ever, I had to tell you even if it meant being rejected again. Rory, marry me quickly, please. I need you.'

He took her wrists and made her sit down in the temple. 'Hey, hey, not so fast, little one. What is all this about? I thought you'd inherited a fortune from your dad.'

She stopped his mouth with a kiss, murmuring, 'Tomorrow, Rory. The English promised not to talk business till tomorrow.' She ran her hands up the back of his head, her fingers in his hair. Gently, his hands caressed her shoulders.

Hardly aware that they moved, they lay down on the carpet of scented, herby grass, and clung to each other murmuring small wordless endearments. The world below them forgotten, they were one with each other, with the stars hung like diamonds in the violet sky; with the ancient pagan gods which stood round them headless but beautiful of body. Time passed unnoticed.

At last she stirred in his arms. Feeling her move, he turned on his side and drew her closer. The night was far advanced and a faint wind rustled the leaves of the wild carob tree which had pushed itself through the stones of the temple. it was cooler, and the shared warmth of their bodies was welcome now.

His voice was drowsy. 'Time to go, acushla! You will be missed, down there.'

She smiled at him. 'On a wedding night, no one will be missed. All the old ones will be drunk by now.'

He chuckled. 'What? Even your mother?' He felt her hand and kissed each of its finger-tips in turn.

'Mama is *never* drunk! But she will have taken a great deal of wine, and brandy and *ouzo,* and eaten far too greedily. So she will not be noticing much, you may be sure. And in the morning she will stay in bed with a headache, like everybody else. Exos weddings are like that. We can stay together till dawn.'

'Woman...' he said softly, 'you have driven me

mad with longing these last three months, and you must not tempt me any more. I'm a man, not a stone god. Either go home or sit up and talk.'

'Talk then. We've so much to talk about. All our lives.' Her voice was suddenly fierce. 'I want so much of you, my darling. I have so much love to give you. I shall demand so much. We shan't be content with small measures, you and I. I want you to make great demands on me, I want to give till it hurts. We shall fight, Rory.'

'Like the devil. At the moment I possess all I ever dreamed of. I hold in my arms a perfect woman, sharing my love and ready to share my life whatever that life may be. Not submissive, but sharing as a partner. I shall have a lioness for a mate. At this moment I want nothing more than to lie here with you like this, on the crushed grass. But I shall make demands too. Some of them may hurt.'

She flung out an arm, as if in surrender. 'Hurt me, then. If I know how to fight, my love will teach me how to be a loser.'

He kissed her, and his tones moved towards passion. 'Evie . . , oh, my Evie !'

Dawn was breaking when Rory woke. Full consciousness came slowly. He felt supremely happy, relaxed in mind and body. His mind wandered unchecked through scenes of the past where he had also been happy. Irish skies, white clouds piled high, the mountains purple in Irish mist; the silver lakes, the fuchsia hedges crimson and violet. Great Atlantic waves crashing in a flurry of white and emerald over the white rocks.

The sun rose and its light came like a sword across the Mediterranean, across the sunbaked earth, the lemon groves, the fig trees, till he was fully awake and knew he held the world in his arms, a woman who loved him, whose lips would seek his gladly. She was still asleep. He cradled her tenderly, touched her hair with his lips.

It was the sight of an eagle, circling high above, that scattered his dreams. He was not in Ireland, but in Exos, and the girl in his arms should have been safely home in her bed hours ago. Island morals were strict, the little priest no fool; and for all her optimistic belief that no one would notice if a young girl went missing all night, he knew different. There was fat to be pulled out of the fire.

He shook her. 'Evie! Wake up! It's morning. Look, the sun's up.'

She turned over, opened her eyes and smiled lazily. 'Rory! Good morning. I love you.'

'And I love you, which is why I want you safely home and in bed before you're missed, if it's not too late already.'

'No one will miss me.'

'That's not the point. You are in my hands and I'm no foolish boy. I do have a sense of responsibility, child. I intend to take care of you for the rest of our lives, and it would be absurd to start by ruining your reputation.'

Her eyes teased him. 'Especially when you haven't?'

'No thanks to you,' he grunted. 'I told you last night I loved you, and my sort of love means taking care of you. Being responsible for you, and for my own behaviour. Come on, upsy-daisy. You're going home now—and fast. Can you get in without waking anybody?'

'Easily. It's too late to go to bed. Are you hungry?'

He thought about it. 'Starving.'

'I'll change into my working dress and get breakfast. Then I'll milk the goats and do the outside work. If everybody gets coffee the minute they begin to stir, they'll be so glad to see it, they won't ask questions.'

'I hope not,' he said grimly. 'I don't fancy a shotgun wedding, with your uncles and cousins holding the guns.'

'Daggers, darling. We are a primitive people when we're roused. You worry too much. Race you down to the beach for a swim!'

They breakfasted on boiled eggs and Evie filled the big coffeepot twice. 'Being in love is hungry work. What do the English eat, do you think?'

'Whatever's going, so long as there's plenty of it. Today's the day they talk business. I'm worried.'

'What about?'

'I figure they'd not send two lawyers from England just for peanuts. There may be a good deal of money involved. Most of it for your mother, but certainly some for you. You may be a rich girl, Evie.'

'So? Money's all right, if it doesn't make a person selfish. There are heaps of things I could do with it. I've thought of some already.'

'You have? God save us, the girl's ahead of me. I'm a poor man. How can I have such a rich wife?'

She stared, astonished. 'Why not? What difference does it make?'

'It could make a difference to me. For one thing, what are people going to think and say? Within a few hours of learning you're rich, I persuade you to marry me.'

Evie laughed. 'Persuade? Who did the persuading? We love each other, don't we?'

'I haven't set foot on the island for three months. I arrive on the same day as the fortune. It looks too neat altogether.'

'But you came for the wedding. It had nothing to do with the English.'

'Who'll believe that? In time, even you might begin to wonder.'

'Take that back! It's a foul thing to say to me.'

'All right, I take it back. But I've seen the power of money and the queer things it can do in families, to people who begin by loving each other and end by hating. I'm afraid of the stuff.'

She came to his side of the table, sat by him and slid her arm round his shoulders. 'Trust me, Rory. It can't be all evil. We can use it for good. All sorts of plans are buzzing in my head. We can sort them out tidily together, after we're married. It's going to be so simple.'

'Is it, dear heart? You don't see problems?'

'There can be no problems if we love enough. Listen to what I've been thinking. Mama will want to move to her little house, and there'll be enough to put on a new roof and add a bathroom of sorts. My father had ours put in, and we're used to it even though the bathwater has to be carried in in buckets. Georgi will go to school if we can persuade him to. If not, he'll live with Mama or with us, as he chooses. If I know Georgi, it'll be both. You and I will live here, and have our guesthouse for lonely people, just as you planned it.'

'As I planned it? I didn't plan a wife, but I'm prepared to modify the original idea.' He dropped a kiss on her ear. 'Go on. Mama and I are furnished with our dreams. What about yours?'

'I get mine. To be your wife, that's all I need. I can manage the housework when the guests come, honestly I can. I'm stronger than I look. We can make extra bedrooms, three or four, by carving up the present rooms which are so big. So we'll be able to have a lot more guests than you at first thought.'

'I don't know that—'

'We'd have to pipe a proper water supply in, and make another lavatory, European-style with a pedestal and a flush. And then I plan to get a girl or two in from the village to scrub floors and such, and install electric light everywhere and buy a big washing machine to do the sheets and tablecloths. You'll see. It will all be splendid.'

'Stop it!' He pushed her aside and leapt to his feet.

Stunned by his furious tone, she gaped at him without comprehension.

'So this is your plan for using your money? I warned you. Don't say I didn't warn you. You mean to buy yourself a husband, buy his dream for a toy, and alter it to suit yourself? I'm to be a tame cat around the house. It won't do, Evie. Forget it all, including the washing machine and the tablecloths. I'm having none of it.'

'B-but it's what you wanted.'

'It is not. I planned something unique, unspoiled, simple and plain. A sort of monastic life, close to natural things and everyone independent and fending for himself. No woman's fuss, like tablecloths. Plain scrubbed boards, and freedom to eat when and where one chose. What you're planning is nothing more than the average small hotel, or a guesthouse. If you think I'll be content with that—'

'All right, all right, have it the way you wanted. I was only trying to help. I was only loving you. Was I wrong to want you to have what you wanted?'

He pressed his hands to his forehead. 'No, no. You meant well, darling. I'm an ungrateful hound, but don't you see—I can't change? All right, I ought to be grateful. But I can't spend the rest of my life being grateful to you, especially for something I never really wanted. It had to be something I did myself. *My* thing, *my* idea.'

'It can't be ours?' she asked piteously. She looked childlike in her misery and his heart smote him for his own unkindness. He ought to surrender, to apologise, to kiss the smile back to her drooping mouth.

He could not. This was important. If he surrendered now, he would be surrendering for the rest of his life, and their marriage would never hold up.

'Ours, yes. Perhaps it could. But you are trying to make it yours, to force your ideas on me. It can't be like this. This is what I was afraid of. It's why I meant to clear off and leave you to sort it out by yourself for a while. Maybe neither of us is mature enough yet, but I'm telling you, sweetheart, this money will come between us, one way or another.'

'It won't. I won't let it. You meant I am the one who isn't mature—yes, you did. Well, I can be mature too. I'm not so eager for money that I will give up the one thing I truly want in order to have it. I won't take a penny of my father's estate. Mama and Georgi can have my share.'

She stood there, feet planted firmly, her proud head flung back, the grey eyes challenging. His heart twisted for the pride he had in her. But he shook his head reluctantly.

'It sounds great, acushla. It would be great ... for a time. For months, even for a few years. But there'd come a time, don't you see, when you'd look at me and wonder. You'd remember what you gave up, to be the maid-of-all-work, chief cook and bottle-washer, to a bunch of no-good, self-pitying, inadequate fellows hiding away from the rough and tumble. Times, you'd hate the house, the work, the men. They won't be grateful chaps, or easy to live with. Few of them will have charm, or even good manners. You'll be slaving away in the heat for embittered, sour types, wondering what I see in them and why we can't get rid of those who don't pay their way. For some won't. Some will batten on us.'

'All right, I choose that. I've sense enough to know marriage isn't all honey.'

'But you'll remember the washing machine and the maids from the village. You'll think of the clothes you might have had; the luxury hotel where you could have been sunbathing, waited on hand and foot. You'll remember you've seen nothing of other countries, never seen the inside of a big transcontinental aircraft or a luxury liner. These things will rankle, as the years go by. Do you think I don't know?'

'But what difference does money make? I didn't have all these things yesterday and never felt the need of them. I don't know.'

'Money. That's the difference. You could have them now. You'd be telling yourself how much you'd given up for me. After a bit, you'd be telling me.'

She uttered a long shuddering sigh. 'It's hopeless, isn't it? If I have the money, you don't want me. If I don't have the money, you still don't want me. I'm beginning to think you never wanted me. That last night was just an interlude for you, and now you're making a big excuse to get out of it.'

'An interlude? Is that what you think? Did it mean nothing to you, then?'

'It meant everything. But to you...?' She began to cry, and although she fought against them, the tears rolled down her face uncontrollably. She snatched a bright orange towel from the terrace rail and blotted her cheeks with it. It smelt of sand and sea and, remembering their morning bathe, she choked with unbearable grief.

'Is it my fault? Am I to blame because there's this damned money come out of the blue? Why are you punishing me for it?'

He stood with his back to her, hands thrust in pockets, staring blindly out over the cliff and the sea. He could see no way out of the situation except by his own surrender. With her father's money, their marriage would be beset by perils. If she gave it up to her mother and Georgi, the moment would come, inevitably, when she would reproach herself, and perhaps him.

'Damn the English lawyers! Why couldn't they have come before, or stayed away altogether? It isn't your fault, Evie. I'm not blaming you, I'm blaming fate.'

'Why not blame yourself? It is you who are making all the trouble, Rory. *Your* scruples, *your* desires, *your* imaginings. Your pride. You hate it, because you're not the one. But if we truly loved, you wouldn't care. You'd laugh and say what did it matter? You won't sink your pride, that's the whole trouble.'

'Oh, for God's sake, don't let's quarrel. It can't be helped, it can't be altered, so we might as well talk sensibly about it. If last night hadn't happened, if I'd not returned to Exos for the wedding, what would you have done now?'

'I don't know exactly. Anna and Peter have invited me to go to London, to stay with their mother. And there's Georgi. Peter will know what to do, and of course Mama will take more notice of Georgi's own ideas, now she's not afraid Father will come home and be cross with her for not educating him. If he still refuses an English education, he could go to Nicosia for a time, I suppose. He ought to see the world, and make a place for himself. It's more important for a boy than for a girl.'

'You'd like to accept the invitation to England?'

'I'd like to go. If we were married, we could go together.'

He was silent. She watched him as he stood with his back to her, not speaking. Thinking. While she waited, she wiped her face with the towel, smoothed her hair with her fingers, found a pair of sandals and slid her feet into them. Time was passing. Before long, the

English couple might be getting up, asking for breakfast, asking for her mother. There wasn't much time to settle matters between Rory and herself.

She had an empty feeling, as if detached from all her previous life and everything she understood. Life not only stood still. It was floating away from her, leaving her completely alone, isolated; no firm ground under her feet, and nothing to cling to.

The worst thing was that she had brought all this trouble on herself. It was she who had insisted on trying to find her father. If she had not interfered, tried to be so clever and managing, none of them would be in this impasse.

It was too late to turn back the clock now; impossible to stop it ticking forward into a future she did not want.

Rory strode towards her, took her hands in a powerful grip. 'Listen to me. There is one way out of all this, if you are brave enough. You said, up in the temple, you wanted me to make demands on you, to ask hard things of you.'

'Because I love you. Yes.'

'I'm going to ask something you'll hate me for, something which will take all the courage you have. I want you to go to England with the Browns. Meet other people, other men. Taste a life away from the island. Find out what it means to have real money of your own. Can you do it?'

'For how long?'

'A year.'

She cried out with the pain of that. 'If you loved me, you couldn't ask it of me.'

'It's because I love you that I can. Evie, understand me. I desire you, I want you with my whole body. But I also love you, and want you with my whole heart. And I can only take you the honest way, by giving you a real chance to choose me because you've seen no one, and nothing, you want more.'

'Who will look after Mama?'

'I will.'

'You'll stay here?'

'The Kyria Julia will have her own ideas. But if you think she needs someone, I will stay on the island a year.'

'I'll go. Because I love you and because I don't understand you. You've asked me and I shall do it, even if it kills me. Only please leave me now, because I haven't any more courage left and I can't say goodbye to you.'

She listened till the sound of his footsteps died away on the hard-baked ground. When she turned back towards the house, she came face to face with Peter.

He wore swimming trunks and sandals. The golden tan went as far as his waist. 'Is there a way down to the sea? I'd like a swim before breakfast, after all that drinking last night. What a party! Did you enjoy it too?'

So there had been no fuss about her absence. 'Very much. I hope your sister isn't too tired. I'll show you the track to the beach. It's steep, I'll come with you if you like.'

His face lit up. 'That would be splendid. Will you swim with me?'

Her throat was dry. She gave an odd, cracked laugh. 'Why not, Peter? Why not?'

CHAPTER EIGHT

AS the plane taxied preparatory to take-off from Nicosia airport, Georgi gripped Evie's hand tightly. He had been wildly excited throughout the journey from Exos to Nicosia. So many new things to see and the prospect of travelling in an aircraft at the end of it all. He had kissed his mother goodbye easily, and raced down to the caique as if he had been going for a morning's fishing. But now realisation had struck him silent and more than a little scared.

It would be a long, unimaginable time before he saw Mama again; before he milked the goats, fed the hens, played with his friends or swam in a warm sea. He did not care for what he had heard of England, and though he liked his new friend Peter Brown, who had taught him a few things he hadn't known about football, he was suspicious of an English school and the English boy, Peter's nephew, who was to be his friend. Friends weren't made like that, to order and because it suited grown-ups. Boys made their own, and it could be this Andrew wouldn't be a friend at all. As for Andrew's school . . .

He tugged Evie's hand. 'Are we off the ground now?'

A first flight is never without its anxieties. Evie hadn't looked. Now she peered out of the thick oval window and reported that the ground was far below. 'That was easy, wasn't it? We never even noticed.'

'Do I *have* to go to Andrew's school?'

'Only for a month. You're going to be a sort of

visitor, and sit with Andrew in his class. The head-master says you needn't do any of the work you can't manage. It's kind of friendly, that's all. He wants you to tell the children about Exos, and our life there.'

'That's so ordinary. They won't want to know.'

'It won't be ordinary to them. You can tell them about the lemons, and dates, and how you want to start growing grapefruit. Peter took a lot of pictures with his cine-camera and the other children will look at them. Then you can explain what's happening on the film. Peter says it's a very up-to-date school with lots of good ideas, and if you like it, you can stay a year, with me.'

'I shan't like it.' Georgi made the mental reser-vation that even if he did like the school he wouldn't admit it. Otherwise he would have to stay there for ever; or a year, which was much the same thing.

Evie didn't say Of course you'll like it! as every-body else had told him till he was sick of hearing the words. Evie understood that it was a long way from home, and terrifyingly strange; and that the plans other people made weren't always as nice as promised.

'Parts of it you'll hate, I expect,' she said comfort-ingly, 'and parts of it I'll hate too. But everybody says it's what Father would have wanted for us, and we mustn't miss the opportunity. No one will guess you're really a businessman with crops to sell, but keep your eyes open for what Britain buys and gather as many ideas as you can.'

'I'll do that. I'm the grower, now my father is dead. The land is mine, so I have to think about business. Will any of the other boys have a business of their own?'

'Not one. I'm sure of that. But don't boast about

it. Just pretend to be a little boy from Exos, and keep the rest to yourself, eh?'

The idea pleased him. He looked out of the window for a while, then decided flying was boring and settled to a pile of comics Evie had bought him at Nicosia airport. Comics were new to him.

Evie had a new paperback to read, but the troubles of the characters loomed less large than her own for the moment. By this time, Rory would have moved into the Villa Julia, as he had promised. He would take care of Mama, do the outside work, harvest the lemons with the help and advice of Julia's friends and relations.

Nothing had been neglected. With incredible speed, it seemed to Evie, all arrangements had been made for the trip to England. Mama had borne up splendidly, under the double blow of her husband's death and the temporary loss of both her children. She had been busy, practical, and happy about their going up to the very last minute, with a new self-confidence which came, Evie suspected, from having money in the bank, security in her own home, and freedom from the unseen presence of a husband whose wishes must be respected and obeyed even when they were not known. She was a woman set free.

But last night Evie had heard her sobbing in her bedroom, and crept in to comfort her.

'I'll stay if you want me, Mama. Everything can be cancelled, even now.'

'No, no, you must go. Your father would have wished it. And if Georgi wishes to stay on after his month, he must stay. I won't stand in your way, either of you. Only be sure he gets enough to eat, and keeps warm in that terrible climate. You, too. You're a good girl, Evie, and I trust you to look after yourself and the boy, but be careful. There are a lot of no-good people in the world. I'm not happy about that languages school paying you all that money. It seems too much.'

'Peter says it's all right. They want someone to teach modern Greek, and that's the proper salary. I can't spend a whole year doing nothing, and after two or three weeks I must find somewhere to live. I can't stay too long with the Browns, kind as they are. Anna says she'll find me a room in a nice hostel for women. Don't worry about me.'

They had clung together for a while, knowing that after all the practical details had been attended to in a reassuring way, there still remained separation.

Georgi was sick towards the end of the journey, bored and fretful. Once over the English coast, dark clouds piled up about them like vast castles and cloud-palaces, hiding the ground. It was raining when they landed.

Anna was there, bustling and cheerful. 'The first thing we must do is go shopping; you'll both need warm clothes, and we'd better buy Georgi's as like Andrew's as possible, then he won't look conspicuous. I've borrowed raincoats for you both, till you can get your own.'

Mrs. Brown welcomed them with a leaping fire, a big pleasant room filled with chrysanthemums, a hot meal. 'Andrew's mum, my daughter Kathy, will be in later. We thought it better the boys shouldn't meet today, when Georgi is tired and perhaps a bit homesick. My dear Evie, I'm so glad to see you. Peter has talked incessantly of you, and I'm glad to repay your mother's hospitality. It was kind of her to keep Anna and Peter for the rest of their holiday. They loved every minute of it.'

'We enjoyed them,' Evie said shyly.

It was true, in a way. Since the wedding day, Evie

had existed on two levels, a strange sort of non-life through which she had walked like a ghost. On the surface, she listened politely to Peter and Anna, showed them the island, swam with them, arranged a fishing trip. Without demur, she allowed arrangements to be made for her visit to England and herself suggested an extension in which she could find some sort of job and fend for herself for a year.

In an odd sort of way, she even enjoyed the whole thing. Peter was a new experience; courteous, with an engaging shyness behind an air of competence and authority, he showed a frank interest in her which was flattering without being in the least alarming. She treated him as if he were another brother, and he seemed content with the role. Sometimes the three of them made expeditions together, but there were times when Anna pleaded letters to write or preferred to lie on the balcony and rest or read.

'You young things get along and exhaust yourselves,' she would say. 'I haven't your energy.'

So Peter was shown all the sights of the island, except for the ruined temple on the headland. Evie could not bring herself to take him there.

But while she went through the motions of a normal life, beneath the surface emotion tore her apart. She lived every hour wrapped in the joy of Rory's love, feeling it around her like a cloak of glory, isolated from the real, solid world like a sleepwalker. There were hours when he was so vividly in her mind that she did not even miss him in the flesh.

There were hours of anguish. Hours when the dream failed her, and she was torn with the hurt of separation. Times when she raged with helpless anger against him, hating him for his cruelty, utterly unable to understand his reasons for sending her away. Why, why had the gods given them love, if they were to throw the gift away? Wouldn't the great gods be angry, and snatch back the gift in their own way?

Once, she went alone in the dark to the temple, but shivered with fear as she moved among the high statues who seemed to loom over her with angry invisible faces. She had meant to sleep the night with her old friends, but their anger terrified her, and she ran all the way home and arrived breathless, and had to make the excuse that she had been chasing a straying goat.

After the week-end, Mr. Brown took her down to his office and explained to her gently all the ins and outs of her father's estate. 'It is not a great fortune, Evie. But if you are reasonably careful, it will give you a modest income for a long time to come. The money has been invested and over the years it has gathered interest. Your mother is provided for, and she has, wisely I think, asked us to administer Georgi's share till he comes of age. So this is all yours. Would you like us to take care of it, and send you a quarterly amount, perhaps? Or do you want it all out, in a lump sum?'

'I don't know yet. It—it seems a great deal to me. But I don't want it. I wish it had all been for Georgi and Mama. It frightens me. Money has power, to change one's life. I don't want my life changing as it has been changed recently.'

He gave her a gentle, half-pitying smile. 'My poor Evie! I'm not surprised you find it bewildering. Take heart, you'll get used to it. Meantime, I congratulate you on your good sense in taking a job. Capital soon thins out if one tries to live on it.'

'My—my friends thought I should stay in England a year, for the experience. It wasn't my idea. I'd rather be at home. But as I'm staying, I must work. It will help make the time pass. It was kind of you to find me the sort of work I can do.'

'Not at all. It's what I'm here for, in a way. We have a client who runs this language school and I telephoned him. I've an idea for Georgi, too. There's a children's television programme which might be interested in him and those films Peter took.'

'He'd love that. He's taken to television in a big way. On Exos we don't have it at all. But then there's always so much to do there. Life in England must be terribly boring for you all. No wonder you need such amusement all the time.'

He coughed and buried his face in his handkerchief. 'That's a new angle on London life. Well now, if you can't make up your mind about a lump sum, I suggest we leave the money where it is for the moment. But there must be some shopping you want to do immediately—clothes and such. You know, I'm really enjoying this. It's not often a lawyer's office gets a breath of fresh air blown through it. Our work is mostly dusty and dull, sometimes sordid. Once in a blue moon, if that, something delightful happens, and a dusty old file comes to life. Now—' he made a move to suggest an end to the interview, 'are you sure there isn't anything else I can do for my favourite client at the moment?'

'There is something.'

Mr. Brown, who had half risen, sat down again, with a quick glance at the clock. 'And that is—?'

'I want you to buy St. Polystemon's skull. I don't mind how much it costs. I want it for Exos. I've written down the name of the monastery, but I don't know how to go about buying the skull.'

'I can't say I've ever bought one before. It might come expensive. Are you sure that's what you want?'

She pressed her hands together earnestly. 'Mr.

Brown, it's what I want more than anything. St. Poly ought to come home. Will you tell them that? He must come home. He can't work miracles where he is.'

'You think he'll do so on Exos?'

'Of course. He'll be at home. We all know him, you see, so we shall trust him, and believe in him. It's in the mind miracles happen, Mr. Brown. Didn't you know that?'

He was silent a moment. 'Yes, I suppose I did. I suppose I've seen miracles happen in the mind. Yet that sort we don't seem to regard as miracles at all.'

Evie opened her eyes wide. 'What other kind are there?'

Anna took her shopping. At first Evie was shocked by the price tags, but soon became enchanted by the gay little garments she found in young boutiques, and lost her excessive caution. The first time she dressed from head to foot in her new things, and went to a hair-stylist suggested by Anna's young secretary, Peter was stunned.

'We must go out, to celebrate. Mother, isn't she marvellous! Didn't I tell you?'

'Yes, dear, you did, many times. And I agree with you. Off you go. Georgi and I are going to watch television.'

Peter chose carefully and Evie enjoyed her evening. Unhappiness, however deep, cannot last for ever, especially when new impressions crowd one upon another. As the English autumn became an English winter with biting winds and driving rain such as she had never dreamed of, Evie gradually began to forget the sharp bite of separation.

Not that she forgot Rory. He was her first thought, on waking; her last thought as she fell asleep. But in the hours between, there were moments when she was happy, interested and ready for fresh experiences and new friends.

Georgi moved into a room prepared for him next to Andrew's, a bus-ride from the Browns. The boys accepted each other philosophically and Georgi, so Andrew reported, wasn't too bad at school, though he had never played football with a proper team and hated standing around in thin shorts and jersey on winter Saturdays.

Evie's room at the ladies' hostel was a narrow slit, one-third of a big bedroom sliced up with wooden partitions. As the latest comer, she had the slice without a window, and often it felt like a trap. But after a long tiresome day with difficult, tongue-tied students at the school, there were times when she was thankful to be enclosed by her own, albeit thin, walls, and to close her own door on the outside world.

She wrote every week to her mother, knowing her news would be passed on, for the most part, to Rory. She touched the paper tenderly, pressing it to her cheek, holding the envelope in her hands; as if by doing so, she could touch Rory's hands.

She saw to it that Georgi wrote too. By an unspoken agreement, neither mentioned the unpleasant moments.

If Evie wrote too much about Peter Brown, it was because he was always there. With him, she visited a theatre for the first time, an orchestral concert, an art gallery, the British Museum where she walked a long time through the Greek rooms.

'Why do you have these things here?' she wondered. 'Why don't you return what you stole?'

'You always see things as black or white,' Peter demurred. 'It isn't like that. The English saw the beauty of these things and saved them from neglect or destruction. We—'

173

Just as the English winter was becoming unbearable, it suddenly blossomed out into Christmas. The shops, the street lights, the absurd gaiety of it all, imposed on the dark and cold, enchanted Evie. She bought extravagant presents for the Browns, for her hostel friends and fellow-tutors at the language school.

The Browns invited brother and sister to spend Christmas with them. Evie accepted gladly, but Georgi was reluctant.

'You said a month, and it will be the end of term soon. That's a lot more than a month, and I want to go home. I want Mama, and I'm sick and tired of this bloody cold.'

'That's not a good word to use.'

'Andrew uses it all the time, at school. So do the other boys. Why can't I go home, Evie?'

'Don't you want to be on television? It's your favourite programme and you'll be able to talk to the people you like. It's what you've done at Andrew's school, telling the children what's going on, in the film.'

'All right, then. But after that, I want to go home. It's a lot more than a month.'

She hugged him. 'I promise you'll go home after the programme. We all keep on finding reasons why you shouldn't go, don't we? The school concert, the T.V. thing, Christmas. We think of ourselves and our convenience, and treat you like a parcel. You'll be home for the new year, that's a promise.'

When the language school closed for the Christmas break, Evie went to the television studios with Georgi. He recorded well, and the producer was pleased. 'That boy's a natural,' he assured Evie. 'We'll use him again. Don't let him go back to Exos yet. We need him.'

In the bus going home, Georgi grizzled miserably, in spite of Evie's assurances that he would go home, come what may, as soon as possible after Christmas. 'Cheer up, small one. The Browns won't want such an unhappy guest for Christmas. Three more days and you'll be hanging your stocking up, and there'll be lots of presents.'

Three days to Christmas. Evie was buoyed up by the hope that Rory would surely write. In the absence of any word from him since she arrived in England, doubt had crept into her love. Surely if he truly loved her he would have sent a letter, even a message in her mother's letters? Had his love been merely pretence after all, his insistence on a year's separation an excuse to get rid of her conveniently?

She had stopped watching for the postman long ago. The sick disappointment every day was too much to bear. But with Christmas so near, there was a chance, and in spite of herself she had begun the daily vigil again. There were still three more days in which to keep hope alive.

Meantime, there was Peter, always kind, cheerful, amusing. She enjoyed being with him, and day by day they discovered much in common, as he opened new doors for her, taught her not only to enjoy but to understand classical music, encouraged her to read with discrimination, to love the theatre.

'I'll miss you, Peter, when I go home,' she said one day when they emerged from a bright, warm art gallery into the dark slush of a December afternoon. 'You stretch my mind.'

'Then why go home? England could be your home, my sweet. I know the climate can be grim, but it's a good place to live. You haven't even seen the country yet, or the coast. Come spring, I plan to show you the Cotswolds, Sussex, Gloucestershire. As yet you've no idea what we can do.'

More than once, since that day, she had repeated

the words to herself, remembering the tone of his voice, the way he had hugged her arm close to his side as they crossed the busy road. Being with Peter had a warmth, a reassurance, a feeling of security. And even an English winter had its compensations.

The morning after the studio visit, Evie found Georgi hot and crimson-faced; he could barely croak a word and his bed was rumpled as if he had tossed all night. Panic-stricken, she ran for Mrs. Brown.

'He's very ill. Ought I send for Mama? What shall I do?'

Mrs. Brown laid an experienced hand on Georgi's forehead. Her heart sank. Christmas on top of them and now a sick child to nurse. The infection would run right through the household, as like as not. But she turned a cheerful face to the frightened girl.

'It's only 'flu, dear. Not to worry. In three days he'll be fine.'

'*Only?* Georgi has never been ill in his life, and you say *only?* It's my fault. I should have let him go home when he begged to. Oh, how I hate England and its horrible climate!'

Her hostess snapped, 'Nonsense, dear. Everybody gets a touch of 'flu from time to time. I assure you it's nothing to panic over. A rest in bed, plenty of nice cool lemon drinks—'

'He needs a doctor. Now, at once.'

'Doctors are very busy with serious illnesses, Evie. We don't trouble them with 'flu if we can possibly help it. I'll keep an eye on him, and if he needs a doctor I'll telephone for Dr. Evans immediately. Haven't you an appointment for your hair? It's the dinner-dance tonight.'

'How can I go, with Georgi so ill? I shan't leave

176

him for a moment. My place is here. Mama wouldn't leave him, and neither shall I.'

'Not *go*? Evie, do you realise how much those tickets cost Peter and how long ago he had to book? He will be bitterly disappointed if you let him down. You have that expensive new dress you bought for the occasion, and I'm perfectly capable of looking after one small boy with 'flu, busy as I am. I don't want to hear any more nonsense about not going. You're dramatising the whole situation.'

Mrs. Brown was exhausted after the long uphill struggle of preparing a family Christmas. She had invited the young Marsdens because Peter had insisted, and because she couldn't see the two strangers spending Christmas far from home, and with only Evie's slit of a bedroom as a base. Kathy might have taken Georgi, but she had no spare bed for his sister, and it seemed unkind to separate the pair. Now her kindly impulse looked like backfiring on her—the boy sick and infectious, the girl in a ridiculously unnecessary panic.

'Why you should treat Peter so unkindly,' she snapped, 'after all his kindness to you, I can't imagine. You're an ungrateful girl.'

Evie's eyes filled with tears. 'I don't mean to be, but everything is strange to me. I've never seen illness like this. My brother is homesick besides, and . . . and so am I.'

'You'd better go home then, both of you. You've never liked it here much, have you?'

'Sometimes I've been happy, but . . . oh, Mrs. Brown, I'm so unhappy now. I'd give the world to be back in Exos, but I *have* to stay.'

'For goodness' sake! Why is it so important?'

'I'm supposed to meet new people, to find out about being rich and all that. Rory said I was ignorant, and in a lot of ways I see I am. It isn't particularly pleasant, being in a place one doesn't want to be, and where one isn't especially welcome. But I promised. Only I can't help wishing I'd never advertised about my father, and that I hadn't any money at all. It was so much happier before.'

'The money bothers you?'

Evie gave a sad, defeated sigh which wrung Mrs. Brown's motherly heart. 'I hate it.'

'Evie, I'm sorry. I'm being horrid to you, but only because I'm tired, and there's still so much to do. Christmas is a bit of a nightmare to a housewife, whatever it is to the others. My bones ache, my feet are killing me, and I'm pretty sure most of the family are going down with 'flu. It can run through a house, once it starts. But I do beg your pardon for snapping. Didn't my husband or Peter tell you you're not all that rich? I mean, did they ever use the word *rich,* or is that your own idea? I'd say you had a useful little nest-egg, but you must realise some people spend the whole of your fortune on—well, on one diamond necklace in Bond Street.'

Evie's eyes opened wide. 'All I've got?'

'And more. Go and look at Bond Street. It would teach you something about what rich means. You'd find something better to spend your money on than wasting it on old skulls.'

'I haven't bought the skull yet. The monks are thinking it over.'

'Look, Evie, I didn't mean to mention this to you, but I think I ought to. Have you considered how you feel towards Peter?'

'What do you mean?'

'Quite plainly, do you love him?'

'I'm in love with someone else. But he—he was the one who sent me away, and he never writes, so—'

'You're beginning to wonder whether he loves you?'

'I can't help wondering. I hate myself for doubting him, but sometimes it gets quite unendurable. I've told myself he'll write for Christmas.'

'And if he doesn't?'

'I think I shall die.'

'No, you won't,' Mrs. Brown said briskly. 'No one ever died of love. Do you know your Shakespeare? *Men have died ... and worms have eaten them, but not for love.* Snap out of it, dear. Here's Peter head over heels in love with you, and if I'm not much mistaken, intending to propose to you this Christmas. Think about Peter. He's a good, loving, thoroughly nice boy, thoughtful and considerate to a degree. He'd make any girl a marvellous husband, though I do say it. Good men don't come two a penny, child.'

'I suppose not. But there's Rory. I love him.'

'I don't doubt it. But remind yourself it takes two to make a marriage. He doesn't sound a good proposition to me. Now, are you going out with Peter tonight, like a sensible, grateful girl?'

'What if he proposes to me? I won't know what to say.'

'Then don't let him. Be a clever girl and keep him off the subject. Don't you know that in these cases the woman always sets the pace; without letting it show, of course? Men like to think they're guiding the horse, but it's the woman who is holding the reins. Use your wits, child. And be kind to my Peter. He's too nice to be hurt.'

Helping with the house, wrapping parcels, running up and downstairs to a fretful Georgi, Evie thought about Peter.

Wasn't it better to have a kind, affectionate husband than a man who could be as cruel as Rory had been to her? Peter's wife would not be bullied, neglected, ignored. There would be no mad quarrels, no hard words. His wife would be a queen in her own home.

A kind man. That was what the island girls prayed for. Wasn't she a fool to go on all this time, yearning after Rory McDermot whose heart was really Clodagh's though he didn't admit it any more?

She dressed for the dinner. The new dress, deep green like seaweed, was a long way from anything she had worn on the island, or was ever likely to wear as Rory's wife.

'You look a dream,' Mr. Brown declared when he came in. 'If I were thirty years younger I'd give that son of mine a run for his money. Oh, by the way, your monks have decided. They'll sell the skull, provided it goes to Exos, and under proper escort, with all due reverence. That means they won't wrap him up and send him by post. He'll have to be fetched. I suppose your priest would organise that?'

'The whole island would go to meet St. Poly. Was there any other mail from Cyprus?'

'Were you expecting some?'

'It's Christmas, Mr. Brown. I can't help hoping for news. Have you time to answer a question?'

'If it's not a long one—I'm due at choir practice soon. We're doing a new anthem for Christmas Day.'

'Could I spend all my money on one thing? Say, a diamond necklace from Bond Street?'

'Easily. I hope you don't want to?'

'No. At least, I might, but I'd never dare wear it. Do you think the money I have would spoil a marriage? If the wife had it, I mean.'

'You mean your own marriage, don't you? My dear

little girl, that is entirely up to you. You'd have to see to it, that it didn't.'

'Thank you,' she said meekly.

Peter was enchanted. 'Do you know, you've paid me more attention tonight than ever before. You always seem so other-worldly, Evie, as if more than half your thoughts were elsewhere. But tonight you are all mine. I hope that means you—you think a little bit more about me than you've done up to now.'

'I think you're kind and sweet, Peter. And terribly good-looking. I have the handsomest escort in the room.'

His hand closed over hers. 'And I the loveliest girl. The day I first saw you, I told Anna you were a knock-out. You've certainly knocked me out, Evie. If I—if I plan a certain Christmas present for you, would you come with me to a jewellers tomorrow, to choose it?'

'You shouldn't be buying a girl jewellery.'

'You're not just any girl. Will you?'

'If Georgi is better. I'm worried about him. I've never seen anybody so ill. I can't remember seeing anybody ill at all, in that way. Couldn't we wait till he's better?'

'If that suits you, dear. After all, it's only 'flu. He'll be up and about by Boxing Day at the latest. I can wait, but not too long.'

She felt a corner had been turned in safety. If, tomorrow, there was no letter; if no word came from Rory, of love, or even a simple greeting, she would know he was trying to put her out of his life. One couldn't hope for ever. She would give him, give herself, one more day; one more chance.

The parcel came late on Christmas Eve. It contained a small icon of St. Polystemon. Evie recognised it at once, for the work of one of the monastery Brothers. She had seen him so often, painting in the small courtyard, lovingly producing these miniature icons for sale; doing his part to earn the money to keep a roof over the monastery and provide the meagre meals he and his brothers ate, year in, year out.

Hands shaking, she riffled through the wrappings looking for a letter. There was only one word—*Rory*.

It was enough. She understood how he had watched the icon slowly grow, day by day. How he packed it, holding it in his hands, smoothing the boy's face, touching the edges because that was where her own hands would hold it.

She kissed the painted lips. 'Thank you, dear sweet St. Poly. It's going to be all right now. We're all going home. All three of us.'

She raced upstairs to tell Georgi. The boy was much better, sitting up in bed reading a comic. 'Honey, listen. We're going home!'

'Both of us? You're coming too? Oh, Evie, I'm so glad. Can Andrew come for the summer holidays? I sort of promised.'

'Anyone you say. You're the master, remember. You'll be twelve, and that's almost a man. From now on, Georgi, nobody is going to bully us into doing what we don't want. *Nobody*!'

'I don't have to be an English boy any more? Actually I'd *much* rather have a grapefruit plantation.'

'Have it. Oh, Georgi, I'm so frighteningly happy. I think I shall burst!'

Peter saw the difference in her. Ordered by his mother to trim the tree, he steered Evie into the drawing-room with him and said at once, 'It's no good, is it? You've heard from him—Rory. Anna warned me he loved you, but we weren't sure whether you were in love with him. I—well, if anything goes wrong for you, I'll be here, just waiting.'

'Peter, you're so *terribly* nice. I almost wish it could have been you, but Rory pierced me to the bone. I didn't know what he meant, when he first said that. It hurts so much to be truly in love, Peter. I don't think you've felt it yet. I didn't pierce you to the bone, did I?'

He bent over the fairylights, knowing the truth must show in his face.

She faced Peter's father. 'I've decided. I need all the money in a lump sum, please.'

He studied her gravely. 'Are you quite sure, Evie? You're doing the right thing? It seems such an extraordinary decision, but you're entitled to do as you please with your share of your father's money. You realise it will leave you penniless when you've carried out all your plans?'

She agreed happily. 'That's what I want, thank you. This is the way I have to do it. And thank you, Mr. Brown. You've been so understanding and kind, all of you. My father was nothing to you but a name on some papers, and you've all taken such a personal interest in Georgi and me.'

'I wish it could have been even more personal, Evie. I wish you could have been my daughter. I'm not blind and I know my boy. Anna warned us the Irishman loved you, but it's human nature to hope, I suppose.'

'Anna knew? But how? I never told her.'

'He knew the colour of your eyes, she said. And that they could change from blue to grey under the sky. Only a man who loves a woman knows a detail like that.'

'You're not angry with me? Have I seemed ungrateful?'

He laughed and gave her a fatherly hug. 'No, love.

The young go where they have to go, and where their stars lead them. Don't think we don't understand. We've all been young ourselves, believe it or not. That Irishman of yours must be a remarkable man! I wish I'd met him.'

She hugged him tightly. 'I wish you'd been my father. I never saw the use of one till now, except to make decisions and give orders. Would he have minded what I'm doing?'

'No. He sold all he possessed in his own country to buy a yacht and go home to Exos. And what are you doing, but going home? You're his daughter, all right. Good luck, small one.'

Saint Polystemon went home in state.

The Exos caique, newly painted, flower-hung, met him at Kyrenia. On board were the monastery Brothers, the village priest, and more islanders than the boat would safely hold. There was Julia, tearful and happy, hugging an excited Georgi.

Evie, carrying the silver casket newly polished, searched the boat with her eyes for Rory McDermot.

He had not come.

Why wasn't he there with the others? Was he so angry that she had come home, without waiting the year he had decreed? Had he already forgotten the island girl, and gone off on a new adventure?

It was impossible to ask someone about Rory, with the crowd chattering away fifty to the dozen, and her mother unable to speak for tears; and Sofia and Marcus at the harbour to see the boat off and full of their news.

Sofia was already expecting her first baby, and bloomed with happiness. 'I hope you've found yourself a rich Englishman, Evie.' The dark eyes flicked over the crisp white-trouser-suit from Harrods. 'All the tourists are wearing those in Nicosia. It makes you look more English than ever. You won't want to stay on the island now. This is just a visit, I suppose?'

'I want to stay for ever. Sofia, tell me quickly. Have you seen Rory?'

'He was in Nicosia before Christmas. He stays with us when he comes. He said your letters were full of that Peter, and what a wonderful time he was giving you in London. Lucky you! Operas, and dancing, and dinners in great hotels. We're all too small for you now, I guess.'

'The Opera once. And only once in a really grand sort of hotel. And—oh, Sofia, you can't imagine how lovely it is to be home again. If only—' Evie cast another longing glance along the quay, hoping to see the one person she wanted.

All the way home to the island, she pressed the saint's casket close to her stomach and prayed hard. Please, please, St. Poly.

Luckily the Mediterranean stayed calm and smooth for the saint's crossing, or the old, overburdened boat must surely have capsized.

As the caique entered the harbour, the cracked bell of the church rang out. Evie searched the waiting, cheering crowd on the quayside.

He was there. Evie's heart soared with joy. She turned to the priest and thrust the relic into his hands. 'You take him ashore. It should be your privilege, Father. You've wanted him all your life.'

Rory clasped her in his arms. 'Welcome home, stranger. You both look uncommonly English! And you look uncommonly beautiful.'

'Are you angry, Rory? I had to come. Georgi has been so ill, but they just laughed. They think that terrible 'flu is nothing at all. I couldn't make them understand the boy has never been ill in his life

185

before. I was terrified! I *had* to bring him home myself.'

A procession had formed, to escort the saint to his new home in the church. Rory nodded towards it. 'You brought more than Georgi home! You've certainly set the whole island by the ears. I hope these old monks didn't charge you too much for the privilege.'

There was a touch of aloofness in him, a distance between them, a reserve in his eyes, his voice.

It will wear off, she reassured herself. We've been separated, grown an extra skin to hide our feelings. Soon we'll be together again and as we were. I feel stiff and shy myself. It will pass.

Not until after the service of thanksgiving, until after the long-drawn-out feast, did she find herself alone with him again.

'We must talk,' he said abruptly. 'Let's go up to the headland. What I need to say can't be said in a crowd, and the talk will clear my head. I'm half drunk with *ouzo*, like everybody else.'

'Why not?' she smiled up at him. 'You're an islander now.'

His face closed, as if the words had chilled him. Fear struck her. She felt a mist of tears before her eyes. Somewhere, in the months that lay between them, she had lost him.

In silence they climbed to the headland. At the top, she stretched out her arms and drew in a deep breath. 'It's good to taste such sweet air. London air isn't for me, Rory. It tastes nasty. So does their water. Ugh! You can't begin to imagine how homesick I've been, for all this.'

'I can begin. I know about homesickness. But I thought you were happy there. In your mother's letters—'

'I'd have written to you, but you never wrote to me and I thought you'd rather I didn't. I wrote long letters telling you how I felt, but they never got posted, Rory. Why didn't you write? I'm not blaming you, just asking.'

'I wanted to give you a chance. To let my image fade in your mind, so that if you came back to me, I'd know you came because you had me in your bones, your heart, and your mind.'

'I had and I have.'

'Your letters were full of Peter.'

'Why not? He was kind to me. So were they all, Rory. If any man could have made me forget you, it might have been Peter. He offered me all he had, but he didn't have the thing I wanted. I tried not to hurt him, but in the end the only kind thing was to leave him. It wasn't fair to him, to stay.'

'You're not going back?'

'Not ever. I'm sorry if I've disappointed you, and I can see I have. You're angry with me. Not terribly angry, just grieved, perhaps. But you're not the same, Rory.' She reached out and touched him. 'What is it? You seem ... different. Has something changed for you? Have you stopped loving me?'

He gripped her hand till it hurt. 'Never. Never that, my heart. But you are a different girl now. You've known what it is to have another man in love with you, you've seen something beyond your island, you've money behind you. What can I give you? The only thing I had, I've—lost.'

'Lost? What have you lost, if you still love me? That's all I want.'

'No, it is not.'

'What do you mean?'

He turned to face her at last, and now she saw the marks of strain on his face. He was like a man who had gone through some private hell of his own. 'For a long time, Evie, I have lived for myself, in a world I created for myself. A selfish world, where I hugged my misery and enjoyed it after my fashion. You broke into that world, bringing me warmth and joy, bringing me to life again. The blood ran in my veins again, I could feel the sun and the wind. You healed the sick places in my mind.'

'I'm glad.' The words were barely a whisper. She was deadly afraid. At the end of what he said, there had to be a *But*!

'No one,' he said harshly, staring out to sea, 'ought to be allowed to love the way you love, Evie. Giving all of yourself, without a glimmer of protection. God knows I tried to protect you, save you from your own generosity, by forcing you to see a bit of the world and taste other fruits before you made a final, irrevocable choice. Because with you, it would be irrevocable.'

'It *is* irrevocable.'

He gripped his hand into a fist, till the knuckles showed white. 'It must not be, Evie. There's something between us now. It's my fault and it can't be cured.'

'It's the money,' she said flatly. 'You still can't accept that. Well, that's over, Rory. Finished. I spent it.'

The shock showed in his face. 'You did what? You couldn't have!'

'You told me I had to learn about being rich. All right, so I learned. Firstly, that what on the island I thought was wealth wasn't really very much at all. Just a nice nest-egg which would last all my life if I was careful and didn't demand too much. Also, that my share was mine alone. Georgi and Mama have theirs. I could do what I liked with my own.'

'So—you spent it? The saint wasn't all that expensive, was he?'

'There were other things. A new caique for my uncles

and cousins. The money is with the boatbuilder, but they're to say what they want. I haven't told them yet. And presents for everybody—a sewing machine for Mama, a London baby-carriage for Sofia. All those will come by sea.'

'The lawyer allowed this?'

'He couldn't stop me. I'm of age. I didn't properly understand that, till he explained. Of course he argued. But I made him understand in the end, and he was sweet about it. He did all the business about the caique, and St. Poly, and—one other thing.' She reached for the small shoulderbag she had brought with her to the headland. 'A rich girl needs a handbag, Rory. But I shan't need it much longer. Look. In a way of speaking, this is your present. A wedding present, if you still want a girl without a *mil* to her name.'

He groaned, 'Don't go on. Listen to me, Evie. There's something—'

'You listen to me first. Then it will be your turn. Because now I've started, I have to finish telling you everything. Mr. Brown, who is wise and kind, told me it would be up to me whether my money came between us or not. And as you couldn't bear it either way, whether I had it or whether I hadn't—I had to find a way of having it and not having it, all at the same time.'

'Did he also tell you how to do that?'

'Oh no. He wasn't wise enough.' She nodded towards the temple behind them. 'They did. The Old Ones. There's wisdom in them, Rory. They've been there thousands of years. Look here.'

She opened a long black case from her handbag. In it, on a velvet bed, sparkled a diamond necklace.

His jaw dropped. 'Good heavens, girl! If those are real, they must have cost thousands.'

'They did. All I had left. I put all my eggs in one basket.'

189

He reached out and took the bauble in his hand. On his tanned skin, it shone like raindrops. 'But why? You'll never be able to wear it. You might lose it. It might be stolen.'

'I don't intend to wear it. Nobody but you will ever know I have it. Don't you see, it's our nest egg? If ever we need money desperately, we have it. If we don't need it, it lies hidden. And if ever the idea of money makes trouble between us, I have my remedy. Quick and easy. Look now.'

She snatched it from him and held it at arm's length over the cliff. 'The island people have always made sacrifices over this rock, to the Old Ones. I have only to open my hand and—it's gone, for ever. Now do you understand?'

He drew a long, quivering breath. 'Put it away, child. You've shaken my nerve. I never heard anything so ridiculous in my life, but I've got to admit you thought it out well. Did you also tell your famous Mr. Brown about the headland?'

'Yes. He tore his hair. He said I was mad, and that he couldn't think of any better solution himself. So if it's only the money that stands between us, there's no need for us to wait any longer, is there?'

He was silent.

'There is more?' she said softly, when he had been silent too long.

'There is more. You mustn't doubt that I love you, heart of corn. I shall love you to my life's end. But there are other things you love, and I can't ask you to sacrifice those things. No, not the money. That's totally unimportant between us.'

'What, then?'

'The island. Your home, your mother and brother.'

'The island? Rory, you're talking in riddles. You're

frightening me. What *is* this? You don't want to marry me after all, is that it?'

'How can I make you understand, my darling, that I have discovered something about myself which is going to make all the difference to the way you think about me?'

Her heart died. 'You love Clodagh still?'

'Not that. But in these past months, I've found out I can't live here. Not for ever. This sea is not my sea. I need the wild roar of a great storm, the crash of water on the rocks. I need the wind blowing off the Atlantic, the smell of gorse and turf. I need the great horses I meant to breed, and my home must be there, in Ireland. A man must go back to his roots, in the latter end.'

'But you still love me?'

'With my life's blood.'

She slid her hand over his clenched fist. 'Then what does it matter where we live? Maybe a man must live where his roots are, but a woman must live where her man is. I understand you, Rory. I think I understood my father. He went home, to England. I don't think he'd ever have stayed here long. If you want to go home, and if you want to take me with you—I'm ready.'

He groaned and snatched her into his arms. 'If I want you! Oh, Evie, you don't know how much! How every day has seemed like a year! How my blood has thirsted for you!'

Her hands cupped his face. 'Foolish, foolish Rory! Of course I know. Why do you think I came back so soon?'

After a long time, she drew away from him. 'Are there mountains in Ireland? High cliffs, and white houses overlooking the sea?'

'Surely.'

'Then I'm safe. I shall take my necklace with me as an insurance. If ever it comes between us, it can go just as easily over some Irish cliff.' She stretched her arm as far as she could reach over the water, and the diamonds flashed again in the sun.

He grabbed her. 'Drop the damned thing, if you care to. Let it go. But you are my dearest possession, and if the old gods took you over that cliff, I'd follow; for my life wouldn't be worth a flea's hide without you.' He began to laugh. 'Darling girl, you take things so literally! I believe you'd really do it.'

'If it were the only way of making you understand I love you, Irishman.'

'I'm convinced. Now it's my turn to do the asking. Princess, will you marry a beggarly Irishman and live with him in the singing hills of Connemara? Because he loves you beyond loving, and will be your liege man of life and limb till death do us part.'

She smiled, and gave him her hand, and he kissed her fingers one by one.